All the Feels

Holly Hamilton

Ukiyoto Publishing

All global publishing rights are held by

Ukiyoto Publishing

Published in 2022

Content Copyright © Holly Hamilton

ISBN 9789360169572

All rights reserved.
No part of this publication may be reproduced, transmitted, or stored in a retrieval system, in any form by any means, electronic, mechanical, photocopying, recording or otherwise, without the prior permission of the publisher.

The moral rights of the author have been asserted.

This is a work of fiction. Names, characters, businesses, places, events, locales, and incidents are either the products of the author's imagination or used in a fictitious manner. Any resemblance to actual persons, living or dead, or actual events is purely coincidental.

This book is sold subject to the condition that it shall not by way of trade or otherwise, be lent, resold, hired out or otherwise circulated, without the publisher's prior consent, in any form of binding or cover other than that in which it is published.

www.ukiyoto.com

To anyone who has struggled with suicidal thoughts or has lost a person to suicide, my thoughts are with you. Your life matters!

Contents

Help!	1
Lending Library	6
The Big Tree	11
Glad I Did!	17
Brit Lit	21
Sick Day	26
My Chaucer	30
Return to School	33
The Zoo	38
Flirting	43
Does it Hurt?	48
Kelly's Challenge	51
Let Your Hair Down	56
Give Up	60
After School	65
Jeremy's House	68
Caged Moths	73
The Girlfriend	78
The Crickets of Vineyard Church	84
Eye of the Storm	89
Red and Blue Lights	93
Interrogation	98
Three Little Notes	103
Did He Do It?	106
The Cleaning Tree	109
Mr. Davis	112
Bait	116
Scarlett Death	121

Sparrows	125
Prepare to Die	128
All the Feels	132
Of Life and Death	138
Jitters	143
The Trial	147
The Ashmore Tree	153
The Funeral	158
Dress Shopping	163
After Prom	168
Graduation Day	175
About the Author	*177*

Help!

Books are oxygen for the literate. For me, there's no other way to breathe. Breathing comes naturally to living organisms. For a nerd with a perfect attendance record and zero friends, air fills my lungs, and words fill my head. I like filling my head with facts, opinions, and fanfiction. There's nothing better than reading Harry Potter and Lord of the Rings fanfics on a Friday night.

Most teenage girls enjoy friends, sleepovers, and boyfriends. I'm not like them. I'm preparing for the future, for college, and for myself. I don't have time to watch the world pass me by. And that's how it goes when you're at the top of your class. Being on top is lonely, but someone must be the strongest, best, and brightest.

The summer has one more lousy weekend. I'm not a fan of summer. My parents work, and we don't go on vacation. The last time we went on vacation, we got a flat tire, and mom yelled from inside the truck. Mom thought a murderer would destroy us all while dad and I changed the tire in the rain.

The rain was falling sideways that day. On summer nights, when the rain falls on its side, I think of dad and how he taught me to change a tire. Mom's yelling is hilarious in retrospect, but at the time, it made me nervous. Her yelling made me never want to go on a family vacation ever again. That was five years ago.

To make up for our lack of vacation rentals, my parents bought us a membership to the neighborhood pool. So, I go every day, by myself. I sit on the side of the pool and read. I read romance novels mostly during the summer. Studying is important too. I'm going to be a senior this fall. I haven't been kissed yet. But it doesn't bother me.

I know that the man I kiss will be the man I say "I do" to. My wedding day will be simple and elegant when the time comes. I'm a sucker for romance novels but having a boyfriend in real life doesn't suit me at all.

Romance novels are enough flirting and kissing for me. My all-time favorite romance book is *The Kissing Booth*. My mother says it's 'below my intelligence.' What can I say? I'm a sucker for kissing and handholding.

Today is the last nice day of summer. I'm looking forward to eraser shavings covering my hands and the endless homework assignments that keep me busy when I come home to an empty house. Everything in that house is empty at night. I like living in the shadows.

'And they all lived happily ever after...the end.'

Another book read from my summer romance reading list. I've read 43 romance novels this summer. Then there's the list of English Lit novels I had to read over the summer. I finished all five of those in the first three days of summer break.

"What are you reading there, Train Tracks?" Kelly Lavender asks.

"My name is Lily...not Train Tracks."

Train Tracks is a lovely nickname the school has blessed me with since my sophomore year. It's a reference to the braces that will never get removed from my mouth. No one wants to kiss a face like mine, and why would they want to? But, when I go off to college in a year, my braces will be removed, and I'll feel like myself again.

Vanity doesn't matter to me. When they call me Cage Face or Train Tracks, I'm reminded of their insecurities, not mine. It's not my fault high school is an episode of Survivor.

When the zombies come crawling for their brains, I will be the last human to remember history. I'm excited to be an oracle and pass down history through oral tradition. You're welcome, peasants. You'll be glad I read it all then.

"I don't care what your name is, really," Kelly says as she rips my romance novel from my hands.

"Give that back. That's my favorite novel."

Kelly moves her arms in all directions keeping my novel from me. Her minions, Alexa, and Tia, watch with giggles flying from their asses.

"I don't think I will. You're gonna have to fight me for it," Kelly teases.

I get up from the lawn chair, and as I do, Tia and Alexa hold me back by both of my arms. Their horseplaying is humiliating and uncalled for.

"You're pathetic. Tell you what, I'm gonna do Train Tracks. I'm going to rip this nerdy shit novel in half."

"Don't...do...that!" I beg.

Kelly rips *The Kissing Booth* novel in half and tosses both halves into opposite ends of the pool.

"Oh...my bad! It looks like the Titanic hit an iceberg. Better watch it, Lily...or you're next."

Alexa and Tia let go of my arms and push me into the pool. From under the water, I see their three ugly shadows move back and forth. I get out of the water.

"How refreshing. You really should come in and join me, girls."

I don't give the KAT trio the satisfaction of getting to me. Kelly rolls her eyes and leads Alexa and Tia away from the pool. I've stopped wondering where the lifeguard is. I'm always picked on during adult swim. Adult swim is when the lifeguard goes away, and the bitches come to play.

An older gentleman fishes out my novel for me. He hands me my soaked copy of *The Kissing Booth*. It's split in two and destroyed. Perfect....just perfect.

"Sorry, I didn't stop them. I thought you were playing a game. Until those ugly girls pushed you in, here you can have my book. It's not a romance book; it's *The History of Pirates*. You might like the chapter on Anne Bonny and Calico Jack."

"Thanks, I think I'll take you up on that. My name's Lily."

"I'm Mr. Davis. Do you go to Ashmore high?"

"Yeah, why?" I ask.

"My son goes there. He'll be a senior this year. His name is Jeremy Davis," Mr. Davis says.

"I don't have friends. I'm afraid I don't know who that is. Thanks again for the book."

"No problem. You take care, and don't let those wenches get you down."

"I'll try to remember that."

I head back to the spot I was originally sitting at before the KAT Trio destroyed my book. I need a new place to read my books. Those girls always find me.

My clothes are soaked. I'm wet down to my underwear. I never go into the pool. My parents only got the membership to get me out of the house. It's worked so far, but the KAT trio has ruined my life at the pool enough this summer. I'm glad it's coming to an end.

Luckily mother forces me to bring a towel with me whenever I come here. So, I dry off and take *The History of Pirates* book with me. On my way home, I stop by the Lending Library.

Our neighborhood has been blessed with a wonderful treasure, the Lending Library. It's the most sacred of treasures for a reader like me. The idea is, I read a book, and when I'm finished, I return it to the Lending

Library for someone else to read. The Lending Library is a large bookshelf that stands on a post. It resembles a mailbox.

I open the doors to the large bookshelf. To my disappointment, there are no books in here today. I put *The History of Pirates* in the Lending Library. Something tells me it belongs here. I double-check the library, and as I do, I find a crumpled-up piece of lined paper.

As I open it, the words on the paper speak to me, they say:

Help. I want to die!

-J. D

My lips quiver as I reread the note repeatedly. I've always counted on the Lending Library to give me wisdom, but it gave me a message today. A message in which someone is crying for help, and I must respond in kind.

Lending Library

I crumple up the suicide note. Whether fake or serious, I need to find out who 'J. D' is. This person, whoever they are, is a mystery. The note feels warm as if it were just placed within the Lending Library.

It must be my mind playing tricks on me. It couldn't have just been placed within the library. And why are all the books missing today? I can usually count on two books being on the shelf.

I placed *The History of Pirates* novel on the library's shelf and shut the doors. The crumpled-up note finds its way into my pool bag.

"Lily, you came back early. And you're soaking wet. We need to get you a bathing suit. Want to get one later this weekend."

Mother, sweet Mother, how I wish you knew I had no friends and that I'm a freak. But you don't. There's no point in mentioning the KAT trio and their bullying. If I can't handle them this year, how the hell will I handle being on my own when college rolls around the corner next fall?

"Actually, mom. I fell in. I'm a klutz. You know what? I'm going to change into my sweats. I ruined my copy of *The Kissing Booth*. Can I have yours?"

Mom comes over and begins her school nurse check on me. My mother used to work at a daycare, and it shows. It's in her DNA to check for bruises and to write 'ouch reports.'

"Mom...I'm fine. Can I have your copy of *The Kissing Booth* or not?"

"Oh, sure, honey. I'm not too fond of that book anyway. You can have mine. Are you sure you don't want a bathing suit?" Mom asks, double-checking.

"The pool closes in two weeks. I'm good. We can go next spring together, okay?"

Mom nods her head and pours herself a large glass of lemonade.

"Want any? I just made it before you got in."

"Sure, thanks, mom. I was wondering if we have any books lying around the house."

I head into the family room and start checking our vast collection of literature. I scan the books up and down. The books aren't alphabetized. There is no method to the madness. The books are scattered sideways, forward, backward, and upside down. I've tried convincing my dad to go digital and get eBooks. But he won't. He's proud of his library. And I can't blame him.

"What do you need books for?" Mom asks, trying to help me.

"The Lending Library has nothing on its shelves. So, I thought we could help. Can I take these Narnia books? Do we really need three sets?"

"No, of course, we don't. Feel free to take any double copies you find. Just make sure nothing is signed by the author. Your dad would have a heart attack."

Nothing like good old dad worrying about his precious book collection. My parents have eighteen bookshelves, overflowing from top to bottom with unread books. Books were donated to them or purchased at yard sales, and some were bought from local bookstores. Books are like rabbits in this house. They multiply by the thousands.

My life has always been about novels and stories. I grew up admiring women wearing glasses. They looked put together and brilliant. So, I decided to become one. I am a nerd through and through. My all-time favorite Disney princess is Belle. Like me, she also reads books and loves libraries. If she were honest, we'd be friends. But alas, she isn't, and I don't have friends. Sometimes I wish I did, but I know they would hold me back with sleepovers and parties. I'm much too clever a girl for all of that.

"Of course, mom. No signed books. Noted."

I blow the dust off several bookshelves. The dust burns my eyes and makes me cough. Why do we have so many novels? I find my parent's old love letters gross. I see a book on psychology and look through all the pages.

The human brain is a complex maze that requires studying and discipline to unlock its depths. And that's when I see it, *'Chapter 17: The Psychology of Suicide.'*

The note in my pool bag haunts me—the ghost letters 'J. D' make me gasp for air. Is it a cry for help, and if so, am I too late? If J.D is dead, is it my fault for not hunting everywhere for them?

Suicide: the act of causing injury or harm to oneself with the intent to die.

I read the definition over and over. The only person I have ever known to die was my grandma. She was eighty-two and had a heart attack. Suicide is complex for me to understand. I'm scared of heights and getting in car accidents because I am very much aware that I am alive and breathing. So why would someone want to end it all?

Are you still here, J.D? If you aren't, could I find your name in an obituary?

I head to the kitchen and check the newspaper. There are no names that match the initials 'J.D.' Maybe the KAT trio made the note up to make me look like a fool.

I collect more books in a reusable grocery bag. The bag is packed and heavy enough for me. I walk outside toward the Lending Library, and I see the KAT trio walking by when I do.

"Train Tracks back for more? You're such a loser. And look, she has a bag full of books for me to rip this time," Kelly laughs.

"Touch my books, and I'll rip your hair out," I warn.

"Are you threatening me, Cage Face? Why are you so weird? You're such a little creep."

Kelly grabs my bag of donated novels and starts to rip it from my shoulder. The reusable bag's seams begin to tear. Instead of fighting her, I let go of the entire bag and watch Kelly fall on her ass to the ground.

I start laughing at Kelly. Tia and Alexa just stand there. They never do anything unless ordered by their beloved Queen B.

"Karma's a bitch isn't she, Kelly. It serves you right. See you in class. And thanks for my novels back."

I grab the bag of novels. Kelly's still recovering from the fall. She's too startled to snap back. So, I used her confusion to make my quick getaway.

I get to the Lending Library and place all my dad's old novels inside. I see another crumpled-up piece of paper. Is it another note?

Dear Lily,

Thanks for receiving my note. Can you help me?

-J. D

My heart pounds. How does this person know my name? And how do they know I am one of the few people to use the Lending Library? Am I being followed? Unlikely, if I were, why would they leave me a note with their handwriting on it?

I take the second note and look around to see if there are any stalkers nearby. Instead, I see a squirrel and three sparrows. Nothing to worry about, I guess. The Lending Library is full, which means my mission is complete. My neighborhood can rest easy, knowing there's new literature to educate them.

I secretly know I'm the only person who cares about the library being full of books. But it's nice to feel like I'm a part of something. So, for now, I'll focus on reading, starting my senior year, and finding out who 'J. D' is.

The Big Tree

The first day of school is always the worst. All the assholes wait outside for the fresh 'meat' they will hit on. Braces are a superpower to keep them both away. Unfortunately, I'm not very pretty, so this first last day will be a cakewalk.

"Lily, are you ready for your last-first day of school?" Mom says, coming into my room with a camera.

"Jesus...woman! Can't you knock? I'm still in my bra?"

I push my mom out of the door. I don't need any more embarrassing photos for the family scrapbook. My parents are dinosaurs with their libraries and photo albums. I love my kindle and praise it like a living deity.

"Sorry, honey. I'm so excited and sad for you."

"What are you sad about?" Crap, why did I ask? It's because I'm leaving.

"You're leaving the nest in a year, and I'm sad. Who's going to hang out with me next year and watch Friday night soap operas?" Mom sobs like a baby.

"Mom, it's okay. And I never watched those shows. I just sat there and read fanfiction. You'll still have dad." I point out.

"Yes. I'll be around, or did you forget?" Dad smirks.

"I know you'll be here. But our Lily won't be here," Mom barks and gets out her camera again. She squeezes my sides. I think I heard a rib pop.

Mom stands at the top of the stairs and takes pictures of me. She gets different angles like I am model material.

"I need to go, Mom. Can't we do this tomorrow?" I ask.

"No, because tomorrow isn't your last-first day. It will be your last-second day, and no one cares about that. The first day of school pictures are the most important."

"Mom, the bus is here. Can I please take the car today?" I ask, knowing I'm the only senior who still takes the bus. How embarrassing.

"No, Lily, we need the car. Dad has the interview for his promotion today. We can't have him being late for that. See you tonight," Mom says.

Dad opens the front door and hands me my sacked lunch. God, a sacked lunch in a brown paper bag. I'm really asking to get punched. I know the KAT trio is a gang of bitches, but they have a point that I'm a loser. Braces, bus on the first day as a senior, and a sacked lunch to boot. I should have played hooky like the cool seniors.

Mom follows me like I forgot something.

"Lily...Lily-kins, wait." God, she called me that in front of everyone. I think I'm going to be sick.

"Yes, mom? What did I forget now?"

"I wanted to take a picture of you with the school bus driver. She's taken you to school since sixth grade. It deserves a place in our album."

"No, it doesn't. I need to go. Bye, mom."

I step my foot onto the bus, and my mom's hand holds me back.

"No, Lily, I am taking that picture. Now! Good morning, Mrs. Norris. Can I take a picture of you and Lily-kins? She's a senior, and it's her last first day ever before college. Can you get out of the bus and take a quick picture?"

I feel the glaring eyes of my peers. The giggles, the laughs, and the comments kill me. Thanks for killing me socially for the entire school year, mother. I did not care about what they thought, but being a senior means I am even more on top and alone. Mom is scaring all future sons-in-law away, and she doesn't even know it.

"Sure, we can take one quick picture."

Crap, why did Mrs. Norris consent to my embarrassment.

"What a loser," Kelly says as she slows down in her fancy Honda.

"Smile...3...2...1!" *Click*! Mom has taken the picture. And I know I've broken the camera. My braces ruin photographs. Why should this one be any different?

"Bye, Lily." Mom waves.

I find my place on the bus. The back row. My phone beeps. It's Instagram. My mom has posted a photo of me and tagged me. I'm sure I'll go viral by noon. To my mom, it's a memory; to me, it's a warrant. I was hoping to avoid the vultures when I got off the bus.

I wait for everyone else to get off the bus. The warning bell has gone off. But I don't care. I can't face the assholes making mean comments about me on Instagram.

Kelly: Lily, the loser. Her braces make her face look like a train station.

Alexa: I know, right.

Tia: Chugga Chugga Chew Chew!!

I hate seeing their names everywhere. If I deleted my Instagram, then my book followers would be disappointed. I'm a bookstagrammar. Meaning people follow me and read my reviews of various novels. It's hard to be a critic. Someone must do it.

"It's time to get off, Lily. I need to get the bus ready to pick up the half-day preschoolers, " Mrs. Norris says.

"Thanks for the ride."

"No problem. And remember, your mom loves you. If you want to delete that photo on Instagram, I won't be offended. That was a little embarrassing. My mother is a strong-willed woman, too. Good luck today."

"Thanks. I'll try to remember that."

I see the vultures pointing and laughing at me. Being on top is lonely. I can do this. I can do this. The KAT trio is waiting to pick on me. Fuck it. I hide behind and tree, and for the first time in my life, I decided to ditch school. Being bullied isn't worth coming to school.

I pick up my feet and run. I've never done anything like this. It's a good thing I'm eighteen. No one can legally harass me about ditching. I know I'll get a detention. But maybe it's worth it. I'll show up and have lunch.

I find the big tree in the park across the street. Harris Park is the best place to be a child. I used to climb to the top of the tree and read books. Well, it seems like a great place to wait for a few hours.

The ladder to get to the top is still there. Three steps up, and I can finally relax.

"Hey, I was here first. Find your own spot." A tall boy I haven't seen before says. His hair is dark, and half of it hangs on his face. His eyes are a faded blue. His nails are nubs. He clearly chews out of a nervous habit. His arms have scratches all over them. They look self-inflicted.

"Oh, sorry. I'm just trying to hide away from school," I confess.

"Well, you've come to the right place. You go to Ashmore too?"

"Yeah, I'm a senior. You?"

"Same. How come I've never seen you before?" The boy asks.

"I try to be invisible. I don't have friends. Not real ones anyway," I reply. I feel like a loser for revealing so much information to a stranger from my supposed high school class.

"I don't have friends either. People suck. I'd prefer the quiet. So, if you don't mind, you can leave now," he yells.

He tries to kick me out of the tree. I hold my own against his foot.

"Here's what's going to happen. I'm going to sit on the highest branch I can climb to, and you can enjoy the comfortable middle section of the tree. Deal?" I ask.

I hold my hand out to shake his. He gets his foot off my arms and helps me up the tree.

"Deal. Get climbing. And I don't want to talk to you. I'm sitting here until school ends," he barks.

"Well, I'm going back at lunch. So, I won't be here long. My name's Lily."

I shake his hand firmly, and he lets go.

"I know who you are. I lied. Nice to meet you, Train Tracks. Your braces aren't as bad as they say. My name's Jeremey. Now get climbing. I don't want to chat."

"Oh, sure. Thanks."

I hate that he knows me. But I don't know him. Our class size is eight hundred strong. I thought I had seen everyone and had eye contact with each one of them. Going to a city-state for high school is intimidating.

I don't look at Jeremey. Instead, I read *The Kissing Booth* and watch the hours tick by. Finally, the bell for lunch goes off, and I tuck my novel in my bag. As I descend the tree, I notice Jeremey writing in a notebook. His handwriting resembles the handwriting on the suicide note.

"Excuse me, Jeremey, I was wondering what's your last name?"

He glares at me, unimpressed.

"Davis. Now go to lunch and never come to this tree again, Lily Green."

His response sends me into shock. Is it possible he's the author of the suicide note? Jeremy Davis, are you 'J. D' or is it all in my head? I climb down the tree and head into the building for lunch. Although, for some reason, I have completely lost my appetite.

Glad I Did!

Lunch is a place of status and friends. I don't possess either of those things. My sacked lunch is in my bag, and I pull it out. As I open it, I see a handwritten note from my mother.

Lily-kins,
Don't forget to take the trash out when you get home.

Love,
Mom

I throw the entire lunch away. Mother's bus photo is enough to make me skip eating altogether. Screw eating a sacked lunch, I want real food and by real food I mean go to a restaurant.

I walk out of the school building unnoticed. No one seems to care that I've skipped school this morning. God only knows what I missed on the first day of *Environmental Science* and *British Literature*. Since I read all the Brit Lit novels over the summer, I doubt I am behind at all.

I walk back to the Harris Park tree. Jeremy Davis is still sitting there writing away in his journal.

"Hey, Jeremy. I'm ditching lunch. Want me to pick anything up for you from *Sammy's Sub Cafe*?"

Jeremy stops writing, and the dark hair covering his face earlier goes to the other side of his face. When both his light blue eyes find mine, he looks like a lost person whose soul is departed beneath the ground. When souls are lost, they speak to me. I can almost hear their silent torment.

"Sure. I'll take a turkey club and hold the mayo. I hate mayonnaise."

"I don't like it either. And you got it. Want a soda?" I ask.

"Sure, Dr. Pepper. Why are you being so nice to me," Jeremy asks?

"I figured you were hungry, and since everyone else in that school is a preying vulture, I had to leave."

I get out my phone and start typing Jeremy's order into my notepad app.

"I don't blame you for ditching. Your mother sounds like a real piece of work. I can't believe she thought posting a photo of her daughter online was a brilliant idea."

My face turns red. My back stiffens with anger. It's not anger towards Jeremy, who clearly has been on Instagram in the last thirty minutes. It's anger towards the woman who birthed me.

"I'm pissed at her if you're wondering. You want to come to the restaurant with me?"

My goosebumps are raised and chilly to the flowing air around them. A hissy cat would be better company than a friendless loser like me.

"Nope. I'm not leaving this tree. If the principal finds me, I'm expelled for ditching. Of course, it's the first day, but still. I'm sure he found out about my summer."

I climb up the tree. Jeremy seems to be letting his guard down for a hot minute. I seize the moment and find myself sitting right next to him in that large comfortable middle section of the tree. It's large enough for the both of us to sit with our legs crossed.

"What the hell? When did you climb into the tree again?"

"You were talking about your summer shenanigans. Please continue."

I ignore his advances to push me out of the tree. He needs to get something off his chest, and since we are both friendless teens at the same school, our respect for each other has grown immensely.

"I try to be a good person. Or at least I tell myself that. But then I get bored, and nothing good ever comes out of my boredom. I played with fire, and let's just say the Vineyard Church fire on Second Street wasn't an accident. The fire got big and hot rather quickly."

"Wait, you did that? Did you burn the church to the ground? That was all over the news. You could get into trouble for that. Don't worry; I won't say anything. It's not my place to come clean. That's on you. You still want that sub sandwich?"

I change the subject to indicate that I'm not here to judge his past. We are two mutual strangers, with no other friends but one another in this crazy instance.

He looks at me and studies my face. His blue eyes gaze up at my hair and my outfit.

"You could be pretty, you know. Why do you have to look like that? And sure, a sub sandwich still sounds good to me."

"You expect me to feed you after an insult like that?" I bark.

"No, I don't. I'll pay for both of us. It's the least I can do for making you feel terrible. I didn't mean it that way. All I'm saying is if you dressed a little differently or wore some make-up, you'd be beautiful."

I want to blush, but boys are stupid. And his compliment sounds like a kindergarten student composed it.

"I'll never be pretty. Not with these train tracks hiding my smile."

"Is that the reason you don't try to look nice?"

The more Jeremy talks, the more I want to punch him for seeing the truth about me. He knows more about me than anyone at that school. He's figured out my whole life from a single conversation, and I find it both off-putting and slightly fantastic.

"It's not the only reason. But yeah, I guess that's right."

Jeremy climbs down the tree, and the scratches on his arm appear. They look like they're healing up. The scabs on the scratch marks look chapped and pink.

He catches my eyes, staring at his forearms and the cuts there. He covers them up with the sleeves of his hoodie. My eyes quickly find his, and the light bluish color has disappeared into a lighter grey. His eyes remind me of a cat, ever-changing and ever observant.

I wonder about all the things Jeremy has witnessed from the top of the big tree. It's his home away from home. What other conclusions has he come up with about the other people in our town? Did I even want to know, perhaps not?

"Don't let the KAT trio get to you. You're a lot smarter than they are."

"How did you know they are bullying me?" I ask.

I thought I was invisible to this school—a living ghost among the healthy student body. However, Jeremy notices quite a bit, or so it would seem.

"I read their comments on Instagram. And I can see and hear a lot from this big ass tree. So, let's go to that Sub Cafe. I'm starving."

Jeremy and I talk about everything. I didn't know an interesting soul existed within the walls of Ashmore Highschool. We've spoken so much; I almost consider him a friend. But, during our entire conversation, I don't mention the Lending Library or the notes I've been finding. For if I did, and it is him reaching out, it might scare him away. And I'm in no place to chase away my new and only friend. But, if the reason I found those notes was to become his friend, then I'm glad I did.

Brit Lit

I block my mother on all social media platforms. My Instagram account has been deleted, all thanks to Jeremy. He deleted it for me at *Sammy's Sub Cafe*.

Our friendship lasted for a day. One day of friendship, and now I miss it. Have I really deprived myself of human contact for no reason? Oh well, I will do better in college. It's only a year of loneliness, and then I will graduate at the top of my class.

I wish I had a reputation to protect. But it's been destroyed by my lack of fashion and having the world's most embarrassing mother.

The only friend I remember having was Maria Arby from Ashmore elementary school. Our friendship lasted for two years, from the fifth to the sixth grade. When middle school started, she got her period before I did. Her social status and popularity grew overnight. She outgrew her training bra, and by the end of sixth grade, she looked like a high school student.

Maria's inner circle was the KAT trio. When Maria became a woman, she didn't need *My Little Pony* anymore. She needed boys, spin-the-bottle, and dating. Sixth graders dated back then, and here I am, a senior who hasn't been kissed yet.

And the period I never got finally appeared in my junior year of high school. Womanhood blesses girls in the sixth grade or later to losers like me. It's a good thing I read a lot of books. I like libraries and hope to work for one as a librarian someday.

Jeremy and I ignore each other for the rest of the week. I'll take his secret about burning down the church to my grave. But, there's more to the story than he lets on. What motive would he have for burning down a well-loved church in a small American farm town? It just doesn't add up to me. It just doesn't seem right.

The scars on his forearms haunt my memories when I think of him. I don't have friends by choice, but Jeremey doesn't have friends because he is dangerous. Or so the KAT trio and vulture club claims.

If Jeremey is so dangerous, why did he understand me more than anyone during our one day together? I suppose we will never hang out again, and I will never get to find out the answer.

My Brit Lit class is awfully slow this morning. I usually enjoy references to Shakespeare. However, today's topic is Geoffrey Chaucer, the famous fourteenth-century writer. He observed people, watched them, and put them into his stories. It reminds me of Jeremey Davis and how he people watches from the perch of his big tree in Harris Park.

"Lily, tell us what you would do if you were Geoffrey Chaucer?"

Crap, I wasn't paying attention. I sure hope I can wing this.

"If I were Geoffrey Chaucer, I wouldn't write about people I know. Watching them is creepy enough. But adding them to his books without their permission bothers me."

My teacher, Mr. Cronkwright, lowers his spectacles and smirks.

"Are you calling Chaucer a creepy man?"

"Yeah, he is a creepy old man. Who does he think he is commenting on people's lives and acting like he knows who they are from a single conversation?"

My eyes find Jeremey's eyes. We both know I am referring to him and his comments about me in the park the other day.

"Did you enjoy reading the *Wife of Bath*?" Mr. Cronkwright asks me.

The truth is that story bored me to tears at the beginning of the summer. I might be a good student and get my work done. But if a piece of literature doesn't interest me, I don't retain the content.

"Not really. I found it rather dull."

Maybe I wasn't supposed to be so honest with my Brit Lit teacher. But I am eighteen, and I'm entitled to an opinion.

"Mr. Davis, if you were Geoffrey Chaucer, how would you use social media?"

Jeremy stares into my soul. I know he is plotting an embarrassing comeback for me.

"Well, for one thing, I wouldn't let people notice that I am observing them. I would do it from a high place. Maybe he would take a video of people and post it later on social media. As for me, if I were Chaucer, I certainly wouldn't let my mom post photos of me online next to my school bus driver."

The KAT trio claps and praises Jeremy for his comments about me. Ironically, he's the one who suggested I deleted Instagram, and now he's being an ass about it in front of all of them.

Jeremy has joined the vulture club. They will lend him a pair of wings and let him soar with the assholes until feeding time is done, and there are no scraps of me left for them to humiliate.

Mr. Cronkwright has no idea what's going on. It's clear by the confusion and blank stares on his eyebrows.

"I am not sure what you're saying. But thank you for sharing, Mr. Davis. Tomorrow we will begin reading *Sir Gawain and the Green Knight*."

I've read about the Green Knight so many times. Jeremy is like the Green Knight. He challenged me in front of everyone. When I accepted, he made me look like the bigger fool.

The bell rings. The first few weeks of school have been slow, friendless, and shitty.

"Lily, can you stick around for a minute? I need to ask you something?" Mr. Cronkwright says.

"Sure."

Being held up by a teacher is a blessing today. It means the KAT trio will leave me alone in the halls, and I can avoid Jeremy. I can't believe my almost only friend turned on me for the vultures.

"The peer tutoring program is starting up again soon. You were the Vice President of the club last year. With college around the corner, I was wondering if you'd be interested in leading the peer tutoring program this fall?"

The last thing I need is to be more involved. I used to think involvement was my ticket to friendship, but it never happened. Maybe I wasn't pretty enough, or perhaps I was too shy.

"That's nice of you to ask. But I'm not really sure if I want more responsibility this year. I'm already in charge of the anime club and creative writing club."

No wonder I don't have friends. I sound like a dork. But I love manga and stories. I wouldn't be me without them. High school sucks all the balls.

"Please, Lily. We need a senior with your grades and expertise to run this program successfully. The principal and I have also decided that the club needed a little change as well. The tutoring club will help tutor the detention kids. That won't be a problem, will it?"

"I haven't agreed to run the club yet, Mr. Cronkwright."

Mr. Cronkwright takes out a dry erase marker and writes the names of the regular detention students on the board. And there as broad as daylight is

Jeremy Davis' name. I don't need more time with that Geoffrey Chaucer wannabe.

He's lucky I don't go turning his ass in for burning the Vineyard church down. Why did he have to tell me that? Is he testing my loyalty? Crap, what if he made the whole thing up? Am I that gullible?

"Okay, Mr. Cronkwright. You've won. I'll do it. I'll be the club president. My only request is that you allow me to assign the partners for the semester."

"Of course. I can allow that for the President of the Peer Tutoring Club."

He pats my back as I turn to leave. I can't help but feel like I've just been conned into a terrible semester of tutoring hell. I guess only time will tell if tutoring the detention rejects is a good idea. I guess one more distraction is all I need to hide the fact that I have no real friends in Ashmore Highschool.

Sick Day

The peer tutoring program is starting up today. I'll need to look my best to teach the freshmen about being a model citizen. Being alone on top is hard. It would be nice to have someone to share my glories with. If Maria Arby didn't become a woman and move away, maybe we'd still be friends.

Sweat rises to my pours like water gushing its way toward a waterfall. Everything aches from my head down to my toenails. As I take a deep breath, I feel the weight of mucus moving around like a motorboat. I sound like the broken wheezy toy from *Toy Story 2*.

Mom steps into the room. With one look of concern, she declares me sick. I never get sick. I take all my vitamins and exercise as my doctor instructs me to do—only people who are stressed and worried become sick.

It sucks that I am one of these people. Ever since mom took that embarrassing photo of me and the KAT trio ripped my book in half, the worrying sunk in. I've never been a worrywart before, but when everything around me is spiraling, of course, I will make myself sick.

"Lily-kins, you're hot. I am keeping you home today. I noticed you blocked me on all your social media accounts unless you deleted them. We can talk about that when you're well, of course. I'll call the school and tell them you're sick."

I stand up and attempt to get an outfit on. Mom takes my clothes out of my hands.

"Mom, staying home isn't necessary. I can take Tylenol. I need to be there today. It's the first day of the peer tutoring program, and they are picking our partners for the semester."

"Oh, Lily-kins nonsense. You're the president of the club. You can tell them tomorrow who you want as your partner. You aren't going anywhere."

I grab a different outfit and start to put it on.

"Lily Green, you are staying home today. Don't argue with your mother. I'll go to the store and pick up your favorite foods if you'd like. Want chocolate pudding and chicken noodle soup? I'm sure you do. Be right back."

I don't argue with mom. When someone is sick, she goes into super mom nurse mode. It's one of the few times I can stand her presence. It's not that I don't care for my mom. She always expects something from me. Her lack of social skills shows, especially when showcasing my embarrassment in front of my peers.

She is always making a spectacle of herself in front of everyone. It's exhausting to keep up with her facades and theatrics. Mom wears so many drama masks. I hardly know who she is underneath. Except when I am sick, all the drama goes away, and she becomes a mom again. Maybe I should stay home so that I can enjoy my real mother on this rare occasion.

If Mr. Chaucer observed my family, he would write a story called the *Wife of Mr. Green*. She could sport her own soap opera if the world presented her with a chance to star in a reality show.

Being sick is the last thing I want right now. It's the last thing anyone wants right now. It's not like I need a break; I just had three months of summer to read romance books by the pool. So why does my body have to give me the day off three weeks into the school year?

The detention students are like their own club. They have their leaders and rejects. Matthew Harrison would be the best student to peer tutor. Dundee Messer is the second in command of the detention rejects. He's like me, a victim of braces. Because he's a bad boy and steals lunch money, the KAT trio and posse wouldn't be caught dead calling Dundee, Train Tracks. So, they stay the hell away from him instead. Smart decision.

Gerald McLaren, another top bad boy on the peer tutoring list. He's a decent basketball player but has the brains of a sheep. He was never an academic genius. I've tutored him the last two years in a row. He was kind and didn't smoke a joint around me like Matthew Harrison did. Tutoring is not my passion, but it certainly looks good on college transcripts.

Out of all the peer tutoring partners, I can pick the one I don't want is the Green Knight, Mr. Jeremy Davis himself. He'd made me feel even worse than I do now.

I reactivate my social media accounts and change my profile picture to an anime character. At least looking like a Pokémon is better than being made fun of. If I get one more *Train Tracks this* or *Train Tracks that* comment online, I will become a single cat lady and skip college altogether.

My fever increases and makes me dizzy. The room spins in every direction. It makes me seasick; my stomach rises and falls with the waves. If an illness is like a current, then I'm fighting it with every ounce of energy I possess.

Eventually, a fighter will break and be forced to rest. The illness is winning the fight, and our struggle is pointless. I surrender to my head cold and fall asleep. The last thing I see is the thermometer reading a high temperature of 102.3 Fahrenheit.

Four hours later, I wake to a table full of jello, pudding, schoolwork, and mom waiting patiently for me to wake up.

"Why do I feel like this," I ask?

"Well, maybe you just got sick. It happens to all of us. Are you stressed out?"

Is mom trying to force me to talk about why I blocked her on my social media platforms?

"If you're wondering why I blocked you on Instagram and everything else. It's because you embarrassed me. I'm already a freak show at that school. Posting a picture of me with the bus driver, are you insane in the brain? What were you thinking? We all know I will never have friends. So yeah, mother dearest, I am stressed. Can you just leave me alone? Thanks for the food."

Mother gets up. She knows I am mad. And nothing she says or does will change the fact that her actions online were uncalled for. She knows I am right. It's one thing to be embarrassed in person, but online is eternal. Being embarrassed online leaves traces. Even if I delete it, some part of its code will digitally remain forever on the dark corners of the web.

"I'll go, Lily-kins. Sorry I embarrass you so much. One last thing. The school called your peer tutoring partner is Jeremy Davis."

Mom closes and the door, and as she does, I feel even worse. Not only did she make me feel like an asshole for telling her the truth. But now I have to be partnered with the school's biggest detention reject, the very asshat who burned down the Vineyard Church, or so he claims, Mr. Jeremy Davis, my biggest rival.

My Chaucer

My fever breaks as the last sweat trickles down my brow. Bubbles form around my pours like crystallized beads. My palms drip with the remaining sweat from my skin.

I twist the cap off my water bottle. It's hard to grab the top of the bottle when my hands are wet from my fever breaking. My mother rips the bottle from my hands and opens it. The water hits my mouth, tongue, and throat. Its refreshing coolness heals the rest of me.

Mom and I don't speak to one another. I'm still embarrassed by her despite my fleeting illness. I have every right to be mad at her. She took my senior year away from me. The KAT trio will tear me to shreds when I return.

"Why did you block me from your social media? I didn't do anything wrong, did I?"

Mom doesn't understand that her actions have caused a backslide in every social event, school function, and senior event from here until graduation day. It's not an exaggeration. It's a fact.

The vultures won't let me live it down. The loser senior with braces has a reputation for taking pictures with the bus driver. I didn't care what they all thought, but now I can think of nothing else.

Did Jeremy Davis mean what he said to me back on our first day by the tree? If I changed my clothes and dressed another way, could I be pretty? Could I be admired and make friends if I stopped being quirky?

Does society expect us to stuff ourselves so far down that we will never come up for a breath of air? Is showing our true colors really so dangerous?

I am scared to face Jeremy. He was so friendly that first day. But, going to school and tutoring the boy with scars on his arms for a semester will take all the patience in the world.

Did he really burn down the Vineyard Church on Second Street? In 5th grade, we had our musical on the stage. Three years after that, I graduated the 8th grade on the platform of that church.

Our town is small, and we are a tight group. Sooner or later, the truth of Jeremy's pyro-maniac behavior will catch up with him. There are only so many suspects to go around in a small town like ours. We might have a large high school with a vast student body, but that's only because everyone in this town goes to the one school provided for miles.

I sometimes feel like a genie in a bottle. But, like a genie is trapped by the space of his bottle, so am I trapped in the hallways of Ashmore Highschool. Only time itself can rub the lamp, set us free, and send us out into the world.

But Jeremy Davis, the boy who was friendly to me for a day, has more coming to him than he knows. He doesn't know it yet. But as my peer student, I am going to make him work. Work until his grades improve and help him graduate. I hate his guts for how English class turned out the other day.

But a boy with severe scratches and bruises up his sleeves has something to hide. I still find it rather odd that I have never met him before. Fate brought us together in Brit Lit to duel it out with words and pen.

I'm a fan of stories and how they transport us to another world with the passport of imagination. The words are the journey that takes me away often from my reality. But, unfortunately, the reality is anything but easy. I get bullied by the KAT trio or ridiculed online when I let reality happen.

Our parents had it easier, and their parents before them. Now bullying is done online with video uploads, secret identities, and hidden usernames. My grandpa got pushed into a locker by a bully once. But it was never uploaded on YouTube for his future grandchildren to watch and stare at.

The internet is eternal. The lies of the inter-web are dark and hold our most hidden secrets. At a moment's notice, any asshole anywhere can find my deleted Instagram video. It might say the video is no more. But we all know the truth, that data lives forever. The world of code is ever-flowing in the spaces that I didn't even know were there.

If I were to predict the future, my gut feeling would tell me that by February, the KAT trio will somehow find my bus driver photo and repost it everywhere. It's what they do. It's who they are. They destroy lives for the sake of popularity, comments, and sex.

I'm good to wait on fame, fortune, and sex. Those things all sound dangerous to me. Whenever I read about celebrities, their lives are hectic, and people bully them daily. We are unaware of the harm it does to them because we don't know them. I've never met Miley Cyrus, and yet we gossip about her personal life.

Why is bullying celebrities considered normal? And bullying John Doe considered harassment and or a crime? Everyone, everyone should be free from bullies.

What about you, Jeremy Davis? Are there people in your life who bully you? Is that why you cut yourself? Did you write the note? And if so, do you really have it in your soul to die? Would you want to kill yourself?

Have you thought about what that would do to your family? Your friends at school? Do you have a friend Jeremy? Do you need one?

I know tutoring the detention reject will take a lot out of me. He is the Geoffrey Chaucer of Ashmore high, forever watching everyone. But sometimes, I wonder who is watching him?

Return to School

Returning to Ashmore high school after a day of being sick is not fun. I miss two days of school, and the amount of homework I have is the equivalent of filling out two or three college applications.

I miss summer. I want to read my favorite novels beside the pool. Sure, summer is boring, and I usually long for it to be over with. But after the strange, terrible start to this school year, I am ready to graduate and be on my way.

"Lily, welcome back. It's not like you to be sick. Are you feeling better?" Mr. Cronkwright says.

I hold my textbooks on my desk. The lead in my pencil is missing. My pencil case has Harry Potter glasses stitched in a pattern on its exterior. It's proof that I am a proud nerd.

"Yes. I am a lot better. I will turn this homework in after the weekend."

Mr. Cronkwright lowers his glasses. His grey-blue eyes show their concern.

"Don't rush your assignments. You were sick for two days. It's Friday, you know. Did your mother tell you that Jeremy Davis is your partner for the peer tutoring program?"

"Yeah, about that? I thought I was the president and had the final say in the matter." I remind him of our arrangement. I was under the impression that presidents of school clubs had certain rights and privileges, but perhaps that is not the case.

"The principal decided that it would be better for the program if he made the partner list himself. And given your lovely display with Mr. Davis in Brit Lit the other day, it's also been decided that you two need to learn how to play nicely."

"No offense, Mr. Cronkwright, but this school sucks. I can't be partnered with Jeremy. He and I don't see eye to eye. We would fight more than tutor. He's a very judgmental person."

"And you're not? In the last thirty seconds, all I've heard from you is your complaints. The decision is final, Lily Green. You may go. Don't forget to meet Jeremy for the tutoring program at 3:15 pm sharp."

I cross my arms as a signal of my inner protest. I would quit being a tutor altogether if it didn't look good on my college applications. But unfortunately, colleges are looking my way now, and my life is an audition to impress them with my involvement and overachievement. Maybe being a detention reject would have been better; at least people would ignore me and expect nothing from me.

Mr. Cronkwright leaves the homeroom classroom. The bell to begin the day dings and rings. I pick up my belongings and head for the front doors of the school.

"Well...well, if it isn't, Train Tracks in motion. Nice Harry Potter pencil case: what are you eleven? If you're looking for Platform Nine and three quarters...Don't bother; they don't accept muggles like you," Kelly smirks while twirling a strand of her curly brown locks in her hand.

Alexa and Tia click their heels with impatience.

"For someone who thinks I'm a nerd...you sure know a lot about *Harry Potter*, yourself there, Kelly."

In fact, in the fifth grade, the KAT trio all dressed up in *Harry Potter* costumes to go to the movie theatre. At the time, the theatre re-released the first two movies for a weekend. They wore their costumes all day at school and cast their spells on our class with their muggle wands, which were chopsticks. It was cute back then, but now Kelly is too cool for the rest of us. She leads the hallways with her oppression and pride.

If a female lioness protects its pride. That's what Kelly is, the alpha lion pouncing and preying on the rest of the school. It's important to never reveal a weakness to a lion. If they find it out, they will devour it with their jaws.

"Watch it, nerd. We heard all about your tutoring program with Jeremy. It's kind of pathetic how you want to be his therapist."

Kelly stomps her foot in place as a means of intimidation. I stomp mine back. I am tired of being her victim. It's about time someone stood up to Kelly.

"I love being a therapist. My schedule is wide open if you're looking for one yourself. How does Monday at four sound Kelly?"

"Is that a threat, Train Tracks?"

"Only if you want it to be." I egg her on because she deserves all the shit to be thrown her way.

"I've been waiting for this day, you know. The moment little Train Tracks grew up and stood up to me. Took you long enough, late bloomer. I will see you Monday at four. And don't forget to ask your mom to bring her camera."

My mother's Instagram photo is going to haunt me for generations to come. At this rate, it will end up in the yearbook. Not that anyone looks at those. But the point is I will go down in history as the Ashmore Highschool reject poster child. And that is the last thing I want.

"See you at four, Kelly."

I walk away. I give her no satisfaction. If I did, it would mean I've lost, and I've exposed my weakness to a lioness. But today, I've worn camouflage and have hidden my true agenda—revenge of the KAT trio.

The rest of Friday is slow. My pencil erases my sketches of castles and Mickey mouse ears. My mechanical pencil has lost its lead a lot today. I fish around in my pencil case and replace the lead. A piece of chewing gum is in my pencil case. I take it out and smack the hell out of it during study hall.

I'm an honor student, and we all know what that means. I get special privileges. Honor students have access to the teacher's lounge. We can help ourselves to their coffee machine and pop supply. I help myself to a Dr. Pepper.

I continue doodling and drawing worlds away from my own. In each class, I doodle and tap my pen. Finally, the last bell rings, and 3:15 pm means it's time for the peer tutoring program.

I'm not ready to see Jeremy Davis. He's the Green Knight, and I am Sir Gawain. But, at some point, we will have another verbal fight. I just know it.

I sit at the table and get out a romance novel. As I turn the pages, the clock ticks louder and louder. It's 3:35 pm. He's not coming. I am going home.

"Where are you going, Lily," Mr. Cronkwright asks?

"I am leaving. Jeremy isn't here. I'll look for him. I think I know where he's hiding."

"Good idea. That's why you are the president of the club. You are willing to go on a hunt for the sake of education. Nothing will stop you from working."

Are adults always this passionate about education? Or is Mr. Cronkwright just this eccentric on purpose?

My backpack is digging into my shoulders. The autumn breeze sways the trees and pushes me back. I walk to the only place Jeremy can be found, the big, large tree at Harris Park.

I climb the ladder, and sure enough, Jeremy is sitting, with tears streaming down his face. His black hair is covering his face.

"Go away. I'm not tutoring today."

He attempts to kick me out of the tree. I get past him and climb to the top where I sat the first day we met.

"What's wrong, Jeremy? Forget the tutoring program. What going on with you?"

Wow, I really do sound like a therapist. Maybe I have different career aspirations after all.

"Why do you care? Just leave. And don't act all innocent. I know you ratted me out."

Now I have no idea what he's talking about. So, I reach for his arm, and I notice fresh blood dripping from his sleeves when I do.

The Zoo

Blood continues to drip down his sleeves. Do I pretend I never saw it? Do I say something?

"You've been hurt. Let me get a few band-aids from my bag. Then, you can help yourself."

I hand Jeremy the band-aids. I pull out my book and begin reading. It's none of my business unless he makes it my business. Jeremy doesn't strike me as the sort to cry out for help. Even if he did want my help, would I be able to give it to him?

"Do you want to go to the zoo with me," Jeremy asks?

"The zoo? Are you serious? What does that have to do with anything?"

"You seem like you need some fun. And I work there."

"You want me to come and watch you work," I ask?

"Yeah. A girl like you needs to let loose."

I don't like that Jeremy sees through all of me. My face betrays me with a blush. Boys are pointless, and I don't need them until college. I'm not even sure why I am blushing.

Jeremy's black hair continues to hide his face. The scars on his arms are hidden under his sleeves. But I know they are there, waiting to tell me the truth. Each scar has a story, name, and origin.

Scars are a part of the human code. It's the law of humankind to have wounds that heal. Some humans have more scars. Some have scars on their bodies, and some are wounds that are hidden deep beneath the catacombs of our very soul. They are all the same, painful at first. Sad to think or talk about.

Is that what it would be like for Jeremy? Would people judge him if he told the world about his scars? Why are they there?

"You're right. I have been a little uptight lately. Let's go to the zoo. I've been dying to see the new aquarium," I reply after some time has passed between us.

"Can you drive us? My license has been revoked. Are you sure you didn't rat me out about the church? You're the only person I ever told that to."

"I didn't do it. I don't rat people out. That's your business to come clean about. I still think you should tell them yourself when you're ready. But I swear I didn't do it. It's not my story to tell, Jeremy."

"Okay...well, sorry for being defensive before. It got ugly for me, and now I have a probation officer, community service, and a record. I'm lucky not to have been placed behind bars."

"Are you sure they didn't find evidence that you were there? Like DNA or something left behind? Maybe you ratted yourself out at the crime scene. Either way, I am glad you aren't in jail."

What the hell am I saying? He's a criminal. He deserves to be behind bars. But then why do I want to know more about the scars on his arms.

"If you're wondering, the zoo is my community service. I have to clean the animal cages. Could you help me with that," Jeremy asks?

Jeremy Davis is asking me for help. Is this the first time he's asked for help? Or is it the second time? If he wrote the suicide note in the Lending Library, then this is the second time he's reached out to me for help.

"Sure. I can help you. But for the record, this won't count as extra credit toward the tutoring program."

I start climbing down the ladder. Jeremy follows behind me. Our rivalry is at a standstill. Perhaps we can become friends after all. The last time I thought we were friends, it lasted for a day, and then he fed me to the vultures the next.

Jeremy follows me to my car. When he stands, he is taller than me by a few inches. I am five foot eight inches tall. He must be five foot ten inches tall. He's putting on a black hoodie, which hides his arms even more. He's like a turtle under all those layers.

He puts his hands in his pockets and cuts himself off from the world even more. By the time we get in the car, his hoodie is over his head like a hat.

"Why were you mean to me in Brit Lit the other day?" I ask after minutes of silence.

Jeremy ignores me. His eyes follow the rise and fall of the electric wire outside.

"Jeremy? Why were you an ass the other day?" I repeat.

"I'm sorry. I wasn't trying to be. It's how I am. I can't explain it."

"It's fine. Are we friends then? Is that even possible?"

"Sure. We can try to be, depending on how this tutoring program turns out."

We arrive at the Ashmore City Zoo. It's a medium-sized zoo with about thirty exhibits and one hundred and sixty animals.

I follow Jeremey through the employee backside of the zoo. The employees call him by name. He hands me a guest volunteer pass and gives me gear to help.

"You weren't kidding when you asked me for help. I wasn't sure if you were serious or not. Okay, where can we start," I ask?

"Let's go to the aquarium. Maybe we can work with the penguins today. I gotta warn you, though, they are smelly," Jeremey says, as a smile stretches across his face.

I've never seen him smile before. He's almost handsome. I wasn't sure happiness existed in a person like Jeremy Davis. He's the closed-off sort, the sort to hide his true colors from the world.

The penguins waddle towards the back door. Jeremy hands me two buckets full of fish. The smell of dead fish hits my eyes, and they water.

"You weren't kidding. This really does smell awful. Although, to be fair, I think it's the dead fish and not the penguins. Look at them in their little tuxedos."

"Those are their feathers, you know. They aren't wearing tuxedos," Jeremey laughs again.

The brighter his spirit becomes, the more I enjoy his company. Then, finally, he takes his hoodie off. A layer of his true self reveals itself to me. Jeremy is like a plant that needs watering to bloom into something extraordinary. Has anyone ever believed in him before? I doubt it.

He rolls up his sleeves, and I see all the scars-the old and new ones. The ugly truth reveals itself to me that somewhere within him, Jeremy Davis wants to die. The tops and bottoms of his forearms are covered in horizontal scars.

His inner war is seen on the battlefield of his skin. I touch his scars with my thumb and feel their bumps and edges without asking. They are all raised like the text of a brail novel.

My eyes begin turning red. The more I touch his scars, the more I want to know. He doesn't say anything. Instead, he lets me study his scars. I count them. I see them. And I know the truth that Jeremy Davis needs my help to save his life.

Our eyes meet. I want to cry on his behalf, and I barely know anything about him other than his Mr. Chaucer disposition. He removes my hands from his scars. I don't ask him questions, and he doesn't say anything. I wipe my tears on my sleeves and start feeding the penguins.

After an hour, Jeremy breaks the silence.

"I didn't always have arms like these."

"It's okay, Jeremy, you don't owe me an explanation. It's your life. I'm just happy I can help you with the penguins today."

"I know. But you're the first person to take an interest in them. And you didn't say anything mean about it to me. So, I appreciate that. Most people think I'm a freak. So, that's why I stay away from the school and sit in that big tree at Harris Park."

Jeremy grabs my hands and holds them firmly. It's not a romantic touch; it's one of affirmation. He needs an authentic touch to guide him back to the sun.

"I'm happy to help, Jeremy. Thanks for telling me. And maybe next time, I can come and join you in the big tree at Harris Park, that is if you won't try to kick me out of it."

"Yeah, sure sounds great."

Jeremy smiles, and this time I see him for what he is, a friend who needs my help. I may not be a professional therapist, and I may not be popular, but today I've proven to Jeremy that I can be me. We both need to survive our senior year together. I can be his friend.

Flirting

Senior year is looking up, and I finally have a friend. So, I guess *Sir Gawain and the Green Knight* won't have to battle it out to the death after all. Instead, perhaps they will sign a treaty and form an alliance.

Our time at the zoo ends, and I have made it through the first inner wall of Jeremy Davis. After that, he will be a maze to walk through. There will be obstacles in my way and hoops to jump through. I only hope that Jeremy is a kind soul with an entire life ahead of him.

"Would you like to help me at the zoo next week?" Jeremy asks sheepishly, like asking his new friend to hang out is a crime.

"Sure. Sounds great. But in return, you will need to study hard and work when I tell you to. That tutoring program is about graduating, and I am going to get you there."

His eyes open to their fullest. They are the biggest I have ever seen them like a tiger focused on the kill.

"I don't think graduating is in the cards for me. But sure, I will do what I can."

"You will graduate. You need to study with me, is all," I say.

He fidgets in his seats with a nervous twitch that sets me on edge. The sweat beside his sideburns falls.

"I won't be around when that happens. I won't be available for graduation day," Jeremy says.

"All you have to do is show up in an ugly costume and get a piece of paper."

"You don't understand. Forget it. I'm not graduating, Lily Green. Can you please just take me home?"

I nod and do as I'm told. Nevertheless, his need to rush home is unsettling.

"Did I do something wrong? I just want to see you succeed like the rest of us."

When I say these words, he stops in his place. He's frozen in time, clinging to my words as if that matters.

"That's just like you, Lily, to care about everyone else but yourself. It's a shame you don't have friends. Accept me, of course. I guess you can call me that now if you'd like. And I meant what I said the other day."

He stares at me and doesn't finish his thought.

"Which part?"

"You'd be gorgeous if you changed your looks a bit."

Something inside me collapses. Not a literal collapse, but one of the nerves pauses at these words.

"Nice try. But we both know a girl like me doesn't amount to much."

"That's not true at all. You amount a great deal. You just don't see it yet. But you will. See you later, Lily. And always keep being yourself for me, okay?"

I'm not sure what Jeremy means by this. Does he want me to stay strong for the both of us? He's relying an awful lot on me for friendship and comfort.

"What do you mean by that," I ask?

He doesn't answer me with his words. He kisses my cheek instead and hugs me from the side.

Jeremy Davis, my peer student, has kissed my cheek and left me speechless. I wasn't expecting that, and now I am more confused than when my dad tried to show me how to use his VHS player. I still, to this day, don't understand how a rectangle can play a single movie on it. Netflix is so much better.

A boy has never kissed me. I am not sure why he kissed me. Does a kiss on the cheek count? Am I overthinking this too much? Does that even matter? When we hang out again, will he try to kiss me for real? Do I want him to kiss me for real? Do I need a breath mint if we kiss sometimes?

No. Boys. Allowed. My girlish flirtations have betrayed me with their desire to get smooched. I don't have time to date anyone, especially someone so heartbroken.

Jeremy doesn't need me to break his heart. He needs me to get him counseling and professional help. He clearly cuts himself. I haven't asked him that yet. I am too scared of sounding like an awful snoop. Is being merely curious a crime in itself? Unclear.

I get home and make popcorn. I read an entire romance novel and reread the kissing scenes. I study couples making out on Netflix rom coms. Is it possible for me to kiss anyone with these train tracks in my mouth?

That nickname sucks. But it feels accurate as my tongue glides along the metal within my mouth. I go on Instagram and see a message from Jeremy come up.

Jeremy: Do you want to get ice cream this weekend?

Me: Sure. Why can't it wait until the zoo?

Jeremy: I suppose it can. But now that I have a friend. We should hang out on weekends.

Me: Yeah, I guess that's true. Sure, let's get some tomorrow.

Jeremy: See you there. Pick me up at noon.

Being friends with Jeremy is going to be complicated. He's going to test my patience and my girlish desires. On the other hand, I don't even know why I think about him so much.

I look down at my arms and imagine scars and bruises all around them. How did he allow himself to think so little of himself? Does he not feel anything anymore? Did he do those to himself, or did someone else?

I start my weekend in the big tree in Harris Park. The tree seems empty without Jeremy in it. It's his refuge and strength. His perch feels like an empty tomb when he is missing.

"Are you looking for me," Jeremy asks?

"No," I lie.

I don't want him to know I was up all night thinking about the scars on his arms. Or the fact that I was studying kissing from Netflix. I haven't always been this pathetic. My genetics and lack of friends made me this way.

"Are you sure? It sure looks like you are looking for me in that tree. Why else would you be up here?"

"Because I have decided that this tree doesn't need you anymore. I'm taking over."

This time I kick him out of the tree, the way he used to kick me out.

"Get out of my tree, Lily."

He pulls my leg hard enough that I fall out of the tree and push him toward the ground in the process. We've landed with Jeremy on top of me. For a moment, we don't say anything. We let a moment pass before he gets off me.

It's then I realize that I've been flirting with Jeremy Davis. This wasn't a part of the plan. The plan was to get him help, not fall for him. I need to stop whatever this is and become me again.

"Are you okay, Lily?"

"Yes, I just think we need to have a more professional relationship. I'm your tutor."

"We were just having a little fun, that's all. So relax. You're allowed to have fun," Jeremy says.

"I don't want to have fun. I need to focus on getting ready for college."

"Everyone needs fun every once in a while. So here, let me show you."

Jeremy Davis closes his eyes and places his lips on mine. And for some reason, I don't push him away. Instead, I close my eyes and kiss him back. Perhaps having a little fun is what we both have needed this whole time.

Does it Hurt?

What is kissing but falling in love with lips? I've never been kissed before. I never knew if I would like it or hate it. So, if kissing Jeremy back means anything, in the least, it means I liked it. Maybe even a little.

"Are you having fun yet?" Jeremy asks.

"It was alright. It's just lip-smacking, at best."

"It's no secret that you've never been kissed before, Lily Green."

As usual, Mr. Chaucer has caught me in an observation. How long has he been watching me, like a guardian angel perched on my shoulder?

"How would you know? Maybe kissing boys is a side business of mine."

Sarcasm was never my best suit. Sure, I can do it, but it always burns the tongue like a ball of fire.

"Come on, Lily. Tell me something real about yourself."

How can he expect me to tell him anything when we both know the scars exist on his arms? They've existed there for a long time. Some are older than others. Some have been cut repeatedly, deeper with each cut.

"Can I ask you something?"

My voice flutters as I ask. A thousand butterflies graze across my rib cage as I wait for his reply.

"Sure."

"Why do you have scars on your arms? Do you have a mean dog at home?" I ask my real question and disguise it with a dumb one following. Of course, it's not a dog. I know that. But I don't want to scare him away.

"Sometimes life gets hard. And I can't feel anything."

"Why is life so hard? I know the KAT trio and their vultures are bullies, but they aren't all like that."

He retracts his body from my questions. I've forced the turtle back into his shell. Then, after opening up to me, he's back to closing himself off again. It's terrifying to see. I've heard stories of people who isolate themselves for weeks before ending it all.

I can't let Jeremy Davis leave this world behind. I haven't known him long. But his parents and family would miss him if he checked out early.

"It's not them. It's stuff at home. Can we not talk about this?"

I don't want to drop it. I want to know about the scars and everything about them. I want to know each scar by name and why he feels nothing.

"Does it hurt? When you...?" I point to my forearms.

"Yes and no. I'm done talking about this," Jeremy says while putting his hoodie over his head. His black hair falls over one eye, and he pulls out a cigarette.

I didn't know Jeremy smoked. Is that how the church was burned down? Was he depressed one afternoon and smoked in the church, or is there more to it than that?

"That's fine. We can be done. But just know, it's not nothing. So, if you ever want help, let me know."

The suicide letter still lives in my bag. If I ever discover it was Jeremy who wrote it, I will cry my eyes out for eternity. We're young and have our whole lives ahead of us. There's no reason for someone my age to die of grief. It's grief they don't understand.

"You can't help me, Lily. But thanks for trying. No one cares about me."

How can I let Jeremy know that he's wrong and that I do care? I care more than I ever have before. Even in our short moments together, I have cared. I have watched, listened, and waited.

"Want to have some fun?" I ask.

"What'd you have in mind?" Jeremy asks as I put my lips on his again.

Maybe I can't save Jeremy Davis. But I can show him, show him that I care. Perhaps we won't date, and that's okay. But his life is worth something. It's worth everything to me to save it. And if I have to kiss him a few times for him to believe it, then I'll kiss him for the rest of the day. *Because to me, Jeremy Davis, you're someone worth saving.*

Kelly's Challenge

The trees blow around in the night. The black night is upon us, and the whispers of the stars hide our secrets.

I've spent the whole day with Jeremy. I don't know his back story despite hanging out, and he doesn't know mine. His life is his own.

"Do you like libraries," Jeremy asks?

I already know Jeremy knows I love books. But, escaping into a world beyond our own is the best feeling in the world. Leaving my life behind to follow characters on their journey is the only way I know how to breathe.

"I love reading. I'm a bit of a romance novel fan and an avid comic book reader."

Jeremy goes into his bag and pulls out old *Batman* comics. He hands them to me.

"I thought you might want to try these. They're my favorite comics."

I take them from him. Our hands accidentally touch. My heart launches into a thousand fireworks. I've started to have these feelings on my journey to healing Jeremy. Feelings of caring for him. Feelings that I've only ever read about in novels.

I need to stuff them down. We don't have time for feelings between each other. He needs my help to graduate, and I can't expect anything in return. Especially a relationship. We are friends, nothing more. I'm his tutor, nothing more.

I wish I had a present to give him in return. I wish I was thoughtful and had novels for him to read. But instead, all I have is an uneaten brownie wrapped in a napkin.

"Would you like to eat this brownie?" I ask, embarrassed at my question.

"Sure. Looks great."

His black hair is removed from his face. When I see his whole face, I like what I see. The eyes of the sky reflect the moon at me. This is who he truly is. If I let him know I like what I see, he'll hide again like a dragon in a cave. When he hides, he might collapse on himself like a broken star.

He eats the brownie in five bites. A scar appears from his hoodie. The oldest of his scars. It's likely to be a permanent tattoo by now. He'll have that on his skin until he dies of old age.

I don't ask about it. Our weekend together has been a roller coaster. A whirlwind of emotions I wasn't ready for. I've smiled, I've laughed, and I've cried.

"I'm glad you like it. I need to go home. I'll see you at the tutoring program tomorrow. I won't go too easy on you."

I find my car keys at the bottom of my backpack. That's the only place they ever seem to exist. I'm like my mom in that way, constantly losing my car keys. Before I head out, Jeremy turns me around.

"Lily, I think you might be right. Maybe we should keep our relationship strictly professional. If that works for you?"

I'm a little off-put by this question. But, of course, it was my idea in the first place. But since then, we've kissed a few times, and I was growing fond of the sensation of his lips on mine.

"Yeah, of course. No problems here," I say, hiding my disappointment.

"So, no hard feelings about the kiss?"

"It's more like kisses. But yeah, we can forget the whole thing. It's like it never happened. As long as we can still be friends and can get through the tutoring program without any issues."

I twist my hair with my finger. It's nice to have something tactile to do while my disappointment takes over.

Jeremy walks me to my car. Everything inside me wants to kiss him again. He's the only boy who's ever kissed me. Of course, it wasn't romantic, but it still felt nice to be seen.

We shake hands. I shut the door of my car. We don't kiss anymore after that. I got to experience one of my romance novels for the weekend. It was nice while it lasted.

Monday comes like uninvited snow. October is cold and wet today. The frost clings to the grass and will be melted away by noon. October doesn't know what it wants. It wants to be warm. It wants to be cool. It wants what it wants.

The KAT trio pulls up next to my car. This is not the welcome committee I had in mind to cone greet me this morning.

"Hi, Train Tracks. We heard about your little weekend make-out sesh with Jeremy. Did your braces scratch his tongue to shreds? I bet kissing you is like kissing a mousetrap. Ouch! How undesirable do you get."

Kelly sits and waits for a reaction to surface on my face. I don't have the energy to fight her. Instead, I begin to cry. A few weary tears covered my face this morning. I don't know how they found out about my kiss with Jeremy. Maybe he told them. I can't accuse him the way he accused me of ratting him out.

I cry because I wanted our kiss to be ours and no one else's. But our weekend fling is over, and I don't want to face that either. Kelly finding out about my kiss is enough to make me sick.

Kelly turns her phone toward me. She has a video of Jeremy and me kissing. God knows what she can use that video for.

"What do you want, Kelly?" I ask in surrender. I give up. She wins. Jeremy wants a platonic professional relationship. For his sake, I need to keep this video from leaking.

"I want you to do my English essays for the rest of the semester. I won't post these videos of you and Jeremy making out in exchange. What will the rest of the school say when they find out that Miss Lily Green made out with the boy who burned the Vineyard church down."

My eyes widen at her final comment. Somehow Kelly knew Jeremy burned the church down. The bitch must have ratted him out to the cops.

"What did you say?" I ask, confirming what I had hoped to be my ears playing their tricks on my brain.

"You heard me. I know all about Jeremy burning the church down. Alexa and Tia were there. We were coming home from a party and saw that freak sneak away from the party. We were all a little drunk and followed his ass to the church. He must have been extra pathetic that night because it looked like he was trying to kill himself. Who does that, honestly? He lit a cigarette at the time, and let's just say we spooked him, and that cigarette went flying. His smoking habit destroyed the church. What an ass, right?"

Kelly can tell by my red cheeks that she's pulled the strings of my anger. She's played to my emotions in a way I am uncomfortable with. But I don't have it in me to tell her that she's right. She's been right about all our stories. She knows the truth about my kiss and his church shenanigans.

"Leave Jeremy and me alone. We didn't do anything to you."

"That's what you think, Lily. I can't wait to see you at 4 pm today to end this once and for all."

I forgot all about Kelly's challenge. I know running away isn't always the answer, but I might be cutting class and going on a long drive around lunch today. Maybe if I'm lucky, Jeremy will come with me.

Let Your Hair Down

By the third period, my stomach aches. I convince Mr. Cronkwright to send me to the nurse. I lie down for the fourth period. The nurse decides to send me home. Bullying is a thing I always shrugged off. It's something my parents don't know about. I have always kept it to myself.

I used to get stomach ulcers in elementary school and middle school. I got used to the acid. Vomit destroyed my throat. The doctors couldn't pinpoint the issue to bullying. I told them my life at school was fine. They blamed it on stress and my attitude to achieve high marks in all my subjects.

My parents sent me to therapy. It didn't help. So, I didn't open up. That's the way it is. If you talk about bullying, something terrible might happen or worse.

Having things get worse is the last place I want to be. But now we are in the age of Instagram, and bullying is eternal in the dark places of the net. I am sure if one dug deep enough, my middle school humiliation photos are everywhere.

The KAT trio now possesses a video of my first kiss. Jeremy would hate me if that leaked. Did he have a hand to play in my humiliation? I'm pretty sure during our conversation, after we made out, he mentioned it being my first kiss. If I thought the bus driver's first day photos were terrible, this is worse. This is the video to end my senior year and make me become a nun...which I was doomed to become anyway.

I drive myself home. I don't go into the house. I go on a walk instead. I walk toward the Lending Library. Another note is crumpled up at the bottom as I open the library.

Dear Lily,

By now, I'm sure you know who is writing these notes. If so, meet me at my favorite spot at 5 pm.

-J. D

It's 4:45 pm. I've missed my challenge with Kelly. She was probably going to egg my car or worse. Glad I miss that. I can't have her recognize me. I grab my mother's sunglasses and put all my hair in a hat. I find a sundress of my mother's. It's tight against my frame and feels like nothing I would ever be comfortable in.

I drive my dad's car. Another unrecognizable vehicle that the KAT trio won't notice.

I drive to Harris Park and park by the playground. The car blends in with the stay-at-home-mom car collection. I walk toward the giant tree, hoping the note is from Jeremy.

The ladder is still at the base of the tree. I climb it and find Jeremy in his favorite perch. If he were an eagle, this would be his nest. His blue-grey eyes meet mine, and I see the ocean within them. If he asked me to jump with him, I think I would trust him.

"I got your note. Are you doing alright? How did you know I would return to the library?"

"Because that's what you do when those girls are mean. You've been doing it for years now. They bully you, and you go to the Lending Library and grab a new book and hideaway in a new world for a while. You act like you are fine, but then your stomach hurts, right? I was like that once too. But then reading *Batman* wasn't enough for me. Getting bullied at school was one thing. It was eight hours of torture. But I didn't have to worry about it under my roof until my parent's divorce. Living with dad has been fine. It's mother and her boyfriends that are the problem. They've hit me and bullied me. So, I decided never to feel anything. I was jealous of you. You just kept reading your books. But that wasn't good enough for me anymore, and so I started cutting. You asked me if it hurt. It did for a while. But I can no longer feel the blood coming out. I can no longer feel anything. I didn't feel anything until you decided to see me. At least, for a brief moment, it felt that way."

This whole time, he's been watching me. Studying my pain when I thought no one gave a shit. We're two bullied teens who somehow came together and united as victims.

"Why me? Why did you notice me, Jeremy? I'm no one."

"I wouldn't say that exactly. You're Lily Green, the smarty pants of the school. I never introduced myself to you because I wasn't popular, smart, or anything. I wasn't a choir member, book club-goer, or volunteer. I was a detention reject. I don't mind my reputation. I'm not a bad guy. I just don't conform to their standards of existing. They talk and act like they accept everyone. But the minute one hair is out of place, they judge you. Detention and this tree were safer than getting bullied. You look nice in that dress, by the way. It makes you look...pretty."

I blush at Jeremy's comment. I take the sunglasses off and let him see my face. He takes the hat out of my hair, and all my hair falls out. It blows in all directions with the wind as it glides down to my shoulders. He's used to seeing it pulled back in a ponytail or bun.

"Wow...you're...gorgeous," he says.

I blush even more as my face turns into a sunburn. Jeremy and I have found each other in a place where only victims can empathize with each other.

The leaves of the big tree are orange and brilliant. They shine with honey and dance with the gentle afternoon breeze. I'm glad I skipped facing Kelly head-on today. The tutoring program went on without us. Today's tutoring lesson was about life itself and that being a victim in this world is cruel.

Jeremy puts my hair behind my ear. I put my hand behind his neck. It seems that our platonic relationship was never meant to be.

Jeremy and I close our eyes and kiss each other as the autumn leaves dance behind us.

Give Up

Bullying feels like a dance between two people. The dance-off is between the bully and the victim. It's hard to see the other people around us if we are bullied.

When Kelly taunts me, her gang of defenders encourages the fight. Alexa and Tia would be nothing without Kelly. What would Kelly be like without them? I sometimes wonder what would happen if it really were just Kelly and I, alone one on one. The world would turn in my favor and shift towards my needs.

That would sure be the day. But it is not today. Not today by any means.

My parents don't know about Jeremy. They don't know that I've kissed a boy. If mom knew it would be in the family scrapbook by now, among my other milestones. Or on some embarrassing Instagram post.

My mind thinks back to Jeremy and the simple kiss we shared. Did it mean anything to him? To me? I am not sure what we are, but it's a good feeling for now.

His story haunts me. How can a mother become violent and snap at their child like that? How was his home safe before the divorce and dangerous after the fact? It doesn't add up.

I'm sad. Sad that he's jealous of my book-reading habits. He's right about me. I escape the world by reading. Don't most people do that every once in a while?

I get out my phone and text Jeremy. I want to make sure he made it home safely. His name appears on my screen before I text him. It's nice to know he's thinking of me too.

Jeremy: Want to go to the zoo with me tomorrow afternoon?

Lily: Sure. We also have tutoring. We shouldn't skip that this time.

Jeremy: Okay, deal. Maybe we can make this a weekly thing.

Lily: I'd like that. Good night.

Jeremy: Night.

"Who are you texting? I haven't seen you smile like that since you finished reading *The Notebook*," Mom says as she steps into my room uninvited.

My mother breathes heavily like she's just run a marathon. Her skunk odor follows her into my room. It's an unsettling smell that makes garbage men cry.

"God, mom! Learn how to knock. You smell awful."

"It was just a little workout."

"Tell that to my mini cactus. Pretty sure it just died from your fumes."

She stands there with her arms crossed. Now that I'm eighteen, I don't have to listen to her petty words of wisdom. There's nothing wise about being a woman who has married into the Green family. I was born into it. I can marry someday in the distant future and rid myself of this last name. I can't wait to shed it like a snake sheds its skin.

It's not that I hate my parents. I despise their lack of noticing me. They didn't notice I got bullied. They blamed it on stress and got me therapy. But it wasn't the root of all my evil. If I tell mom I have a fling with Jeremy Davis, she will want to know more.

If she knows more, she might discover his smoking habit and the scars that come with him. Jeremy and I are not so different in our bullying. The only difference is his pain took him further. It took him to cutting.

I don't have it in me to cut. Taking a knife and harming myself doesn't make sense. I don't understand it.

"Who is it, honey," Mom asks again?

I forgot she was here in the room for a split second. Thinking about Jeremy is distracting.

"It was my tutoring student, Jeremy Davis. He needed help with his homework."

"Then why were you laughing? You look more like a giddy woman to me."

"Oh, mom! No. Gross. Come on."

This conversation just keeps getting better and better. Mom sure knows how to make me not want to talk to her.

"Now leave. You stink. I'm going to have to open up all the windows again. Seriously why can't you wear deodorant like a normal person?"

"There's aluminum in that stuff. I don't know if that's FDA approved," mom says as she lifts her arms and smells herself in front of me. My eyes burn from her skunk-like presence.

"Then find an alternative and start using it."

I grab her by her sweaty arm and shove her out of my room. She staggers a bit when I do. I lock the door as soon as she's in the hallway.

Besides our love of reading books, my mother and I are from opposite sides of the galaxy. I want to be invisible, and she wants all the attention one might receive as a contestant on *America's Got Talent*.

The morning finds me like it always does. This morning I make coffee and take my dad's car without asking. An inner rebel is forming, and it doesn't scare me in the least. Perhaps being overly protective towards me their whole life has changed me into the adult I've always wanted to be. I'm young and free as a bird in the air.

I drive to Jeremy's house. His black hair has been cut. He's had the sides buzzed off and has left a bit of hair in the top. Something about it makes the colony of butterflies migrate toward my face.

He has a highlighter in his hand. He's busy studying something, and I can't make out what it is.

"What are you highlighting?"

"Jobs in the newspaper. If I don't graduate, I need something to keep me busy," he replies as his grey eyes stare into mine. His stare is as intense as a wolf searching for a purpose.

"Can you look online," I ask?

"I don't have internet. I have to use my phone's cellular data for schoolwork."

It never occurred to me that some people still don't have internet in this country. When I think about a lack of internet access, I think of developing countries. Not the USA.

"If you need internet, I would be happy to have you study at my house. Or I could take you to the library sometime."

He nods his head as a sign of agreement. Maybe I offered because I want more time with the boy with scars on his arms deep down.

We get to school and part ways. It was nice to have Jeremy in my car. It's nice to know we will go to the zoo later.

Gerald McLaren stops in front of my locker. He's one of the other detention rejects. He's started to gain popularity as Kelly's boyfriend.

"Why didn't you show up the other day at 4 pm? Kelly's not pleased."

"So, what? Let her get used to disappointment. Something came up."

"She has a message for you. She plans on leaking the news about Jeremy burning down the church sometime today unless you confront her and reconsider her challenge."

"I'll think about it," I say.

Gerald McLaren looks like a dumbass. Instead, he resembles a dopey giant with missing teeth. He's lost all his brain cells from all the joints he's smoked.

Lily: Jeremy, I can't go to the zoo today. Something has come up.

I can't tell Jeremy that it was Kelly who ratted him out. Because if I do, it will be all over Instagram. I have to protect him from the KAT trio and further depression.

Jeremy: What's come up?

Lily: Parents are asshats.

I know it's a lie. But it's still better than him knowing the truth that I am fighting his battles for him. So after school today, I will be squashed like a bug, all to protect the fling that I have with the detention reject, Jeremy Davis.

After School

I spend the day worrying about Jeremy. I check my phone every class to make sure all social media platforms are clear of his church burning news.

The fly on the wall is watching me with his millions of eyes. Those eyes follow me everywhere. If one hair is out of place, Kelly will either post our first kiss video, or she will let the school know Jeremy is a pyromaniac. Either way, she wins. She's on top, like the Bitch Queen of the Nile.

"What have you decided, Train Tracks? It's embarrassing either way. Either let me have my fun after school, or you and Jeremy can be an embarrassing couple of Instagram, or he can just go to prison now. The choice is yours, really."

Kelly taps her foot and crosses her arms. Her lips smack with the sound of her chewing gum. She tilts her neck and smirks her lips. She's fierce.

"I'll see you after school," I reply, not knowing what else to do or say. Saying anything to stop her is pointless. If I were a witch, I'd cast a spell on her, and she'd be invisible or turned into a mosquito.

"Good choice and don't be late. You might want to come along. Meet me by the big tree in Harris Park."

When I hear where she wants to meet, it feels like a violation. Not a violation of my property, but Jeremy's. They've discovered his most sacred space and are taking it away from him. I can only imagine the things they will do.

I throw my sacked lunch away. Food is the last thing I need before having the bullies force it all out of me with their actions. I don't know if Kelly can break my will, but I know she'll try.

Each class is agony. One more hour to my doom. One more hour until I take the fall for Jeremy. How many scars will he not carve into himself if I do this for him?

I leave everything in my backpack. Kelly won't make a skeptical out of my belongings. She can't destroy my things if she doesn't know my locker combination.

The walk to Harris Park feels like the walk Aslan, the lion from Narnia, made for Edmund. He sacrificed himself for Edmund and gave himself up to the White Witch, or so the story goes. My dad used to read me that story besides the fireplace. Then, after mom went to bed, it was just him and me and Narnia.

The big tree is empty. Jeremy must have left school earlier because I rejected him. I sure hope he isn't too pissed at me.

The grass shuffles behind me as eight pairs of feet stand behind me. Four hideous hyenas bark their laughs toward me.

Tia and Amy hold up their phones and begin taking a video. Kelly and Gerald approach me. She's walking toward me like Cersei Lannister from *Game of Thrones*. She stands tall with her posture carrying her about the park. Cersei had her tall protector, The Mountain, at her beck and call. Gerald McLaren is as tall, loyal, and stupid as The Mountain.

"Hello, Instagrammers and Nerd Haters. It's me, Kelly. Today I'm going to show you how to deal with a loser. First, you buy a carton full of eggs. Then you open the carton of eggs, and one by one, you throw them at the asshole who spreads rumors about you online."

Kelly and Gerald throw eggs at me. They crack and break against my forehead, arms, and chest. I feel the snot of all the egg yolks dripping down my face. My eyes turn pink. I can't tell if it's from the egg yolk burning, the phone cameras rolling, or Kelly laughing and humiliating me. But either way, Jeremy is safe for one more day.

Kelly's hand finds the back of my head. She lifts the camera and shows everyone my egg-stained face. Tia and Amy are cracking up at the example

Kelly has made of me. I've become a laughingstock like a fifteenth-century criminal put on display for crowds to throw food at.

Next, Kelly brings out the spray paint and begins spray painting the big tree. She sprays the inside where Jeremy likes to sit. They cut the ladder down. They take the ladder with them and leave me alone at the base of the tree.

My body shakes from the torture. This is far worse than a picture that my mom posted online. I will forever be the star of the egg yolk prank.

And just when I think it's over, Kelly dumps a large five-pound bag of flour over my head.

"And that's how you stop a loser. For any questions or comments, please feel free to reach out to me, Kelly. The real victim here."

What a bitch. I can't believe she called herself the victim. Kelly laughs and pulls my hair.

"This was fun, Train Tracks. I hope we can do it again sometime. Are those tears? Don't bother crying, loser. It will only get worse from here. And I'd watch that little boyfriend of yours. Sooner or later, something bad just might happen. In the meantime, you better keep writing all my papers for the rest of the year."

She pushes me into the tree. Tia and Amy get into Gerald's car. All four of them drive away, and the last thing I see is Kelly flipping me off in the front passenger's seat.

Jeremy's House

Egg yolk and flour mix in clumps all over me. This is how an unmixed pancake must feel. I don't know how I am going to scrape all this off. Good thing I left my backpack in my locker. The school is closed. I'll have to get my phone later. And I think my keys are in there too. Perfect, just perfect.

I wish I had been with Jeremy at the zoo. We could have been swimming with the dolphins by now. The base of the big tree has one spot left, one spot left where they didn't paint all over it. I don't know how Kelly and her posse managed to get away with graffiti in broad daylight. She probably started the fire in the church and somehow framed Jeremy for it. Maybe I should visit the ruins of the Vineyard Church and do some digging for the truth myself.

I cry under the base of the tree. The snot of the egg yolk and flour dust make me cough. I can barely see through either substance.

A loud car muffler stops a few meters away from the big tree. I wonder if people have paid for tickets to see my humiliated state.

"Lily-kins, is that you? My God, what happened?" It's my mom's voice.

For the first time in my life, my mother has discovered me as a victim of bullying. I must look even more pathetic. Here I am, eighteen years old, and I look like I've had my ass kicked.

"Hey, mom. Can... you...not ask...about this? I want to...go...home," I say through egg yolk dripping down my head and flour dusting my body.

For once, mom doesn't overstep. She doesn't say anything. Instead, she opens the car door and acts like a real mother.

"Mom, can you go into the school and get my backpack from my locker? My phone's in there. I'm sure a janitor will let you in."

Mom parks right by the school. Mr. Evans, a small gentleman with a large bushy beard, lets her in. He follows her inside. I'm sure he'll open the locker with a key or something.

I search around the car for something to wash my face off with. An old water bottle that hasn't been opened before lies under the driver's seat. I stretch out my feet and grab them. In the school's parking lot, I pour water all over my face. Finally, my eyes are free from their cake mix prison.

Mom and Mr. Cronkwright walk out of the school side by side. He takes one look at me and understands why I haven't been at the tutoring program.

"Lily...my...gods. Is this why you didn't come to tutoring? What the hell happened," Mr. Cronkwright asks?

I get back in the car and ignore the interrogation. Mom told a teacher. Great, just great.

"Are you being bullied," Mom asks?

"Mom... I'm...not...talking...about...this...now."

How humiliating she had to get a teacher involved. I know it means she cares. But the last thing I want to do is face the truth an hour after it's happened. Maybe if I had been allowed to rest this weekend, I would have been open to a bullying dialogue later. But now, I have no interest. Thank God, I am eighteen.

I rip my backpack from her arms and don't get in the car with her.

"Lily-kins, get back here."

I ignore my mom and Mr. Cronkwright. I ignore them all. I get in my car and drive myself to Jeremy's house. I'm not sure what I might find at

Jeremy's house. Perhaps he'll be waiting for me to apologize for skipping the zoo. Maybe he could be on Instagram, watching Kelly's video of my humiliation. If he is, he'll realize that I've reached an edge.

Anger dwells within my body like a serpent sitting in a cave. When the prey approaches the entrance, the cobra strikes, and its fangs of poison bite down and waits for the target to stop breathing.

Today, Kelly was the cobra, and her fangs have bitten me. Fangs are deep when they puncture the skin. Then, they sink further into the flesh until the poison reaches the veins. Veins are the map way of the body, stretching from system to system. And when it's done, the poison kills the animal, and it stops breathing. So, Kelly's cobra venom is transforming me into my version of a cobra with an appetite for revenge. Revenge to take out the KAT trio.

It's hard to drive with eggs sticking to my body. Also, my car will need a good vacuuming out after all this flour has been on my driver's seat. The white powder almost feels like sand against the skin on my back.

Jeremy's house has a yellow car parked in front. It can't be Jeremy's car. He isn't allowed to drive. He has a criminal record, the one I suspect Kelly is actually responsible for.

The house's curtains are pulled to the side by a familiar hand. Jeremy stares at me through the window. Then, he rushes to the door.

"What the hell happened," he asks?

"Can I take a shower here? I really don't want to talk about it."

He takes my hand and leads me upstairs. There's so much egg mucus and flour dust that I cannot decipher if there is new blood on Jeremy's arm. He seems to be cutting himself more and more. The deeper he cuts, the further he falls into the void.

The void is where the two yellow eyes live. The ones that pull us down into depression with their claws. Depression is a devouring monster. He's always hungry and never rests. His sleepless nights make the world a restless, anxious place to be in.

Jeremy turns the shower on and warms the water up. He hands me some of his old sweats and a large black hoodie. The hoodie has an anime character on it, a large Pikachu.

"Nice Pokémon sweater. I love it. "

"Yeah, I grew up playing the card game and watching that show with my dad," Jeremy adds with a fondness I've never seen before.

He hands me a Pokémon beach towel, and I giggle a little as I see it. It's the first time I've laughed even a little since I was bullied. He really is medication for the soul, and he is too stressed with his own life to notice he is healing me.

"I'll be making nachos while you're in the shower. Want me to make you some for when you get out," Jeremy asks?

I nod my head in a daze. Jeremy seems to have no interest in the fact that I am about to become naked in his house. It's nice to be ignored right now. I can only imagine all the attention I'm getting online right now as we speak.

Jeremy heads downstairs as I lock the door. For a young man, his bathroom is spotless. It's tidy and clean...too clean. Like someone is trying to hide a truth. The horrible truth is that Jeremy cuts his arms.

I poke around in the bottom of Jeremy's sink and find rubbing alcohol and evidence of fresh blood. There's Kleenex in the trash of red blood. It looks new like he's just done it. A knife with a serrated blade rests in the bottom drawer of the bathroom. It was wiped clean, but not good enough. Fresh blood drips on the blade. Again, he's just done this. I can't acknowledge this today. I have to clean up my trauma first.

I climb into the shower. The eggshells fall out of my hair, and yellow egg yolks fall in clumps. I wash my hair three times with shampoo. The flour finally comes out. My silent tears are interrupted by a knock at the door.

"Are you okay in there? Your nachos are done."

I turn the water off. I take a deep breath. The fluffy Pikachu towel soon dries me off. His clothes are huge on me but are better than any clothes I'd have at home for a time like this.

"Yes, I'm fine. Nachos sound good. I have a lot to tell you."

Jeremy and I eat nachos. We talk about Kelly. We watch the Instagram video that was posted. After this day, we decide to leave social media for the rest of the school year. As we both delete our social media accounts, a thought comes over me. That we have just taken Kelly's social media powers away from us, and that is a victory worth celebrating.

Caged Moths

A house is where people live and have a hard time connecting. A home is where a person feels safe. Right now, Jeremy feels like that to me. So, he took me in and let me be myself.

"Lily, at some point, we are going to have to face them, you know," Jeremy asks?

My thoughts linger for a moment before catching up to me. I will have to get in the car and leave Jeremy's house at some point.

"I know. I'm not ready to think about them right now. The KAT trio will be taken out. It's inevitable. Jeremy, can I stay here a little while longer," I ask?

I'd do anything to stay here and look at Jeremy. But, in my desire to be safe, I've found I want to keep him safe from the demons that live within his soul. His soul is tainted by monsters. Monsters have the faces of everyday people. They live where people are ghouls, and ghouls look like good guys.

"Sure, you can probably stay and watch a movie," Jeremy says as he finishes the rest of his nachos.

I nibble on my nachos and taste the salty staleness beneath my tongue.

"No, Jeremy. Can I stay for the weekend? I kind of ran away from my mom and Mr. Cronkwright. They both saw me looking like a snotty ghost. And I don't want to be interviewed by my mom right now. I am mad at her and my dad to tell you the truth. They never noticed anything. They saw what they wanted to see. They never saw the bullying until it became real to their eyes. I hate them. I hate all of them. I hate Amy's phone for taking pictures. I hate Tia for laughing. But, above all, I HATE KELLY. Why does she have to be such a bitch to me? I didn't...do...anything.

They...make...me...want to...run...away. They make me want to...scream until...I am no more..."

I stop talking; the words are gone. I have no more words left to fill the air with. A nearby dog outside barks as two cyclists pass by.

"Lily, are you okay?"

The tears form in my eyes—the windows to my soul collapse. I can't save Jeremy if I am battling my ghouls. I wish I could climb out of my hole, so I can keep you safe, Jeremy. But I... don't know why I feel this way. Maybe, I've felt it since that day in the tree when he noticed me in his perch.

"No, I'm not okay. I'm scared of them. Scared of what they'll do to me. What they might do to you. I can't let that happen. I won't."

A lump forms in my throat. The dryness in the air makes it hard to swallow. My mouth can't make saliva because I'm dehydrated. Jeremy hands me his water bottle, and I take a sip.

I'm embarrassed because somewhere between the bullying, the crying, and fear for Jeremy's life, I've fallen for him. I've fallen for him in the way I've read about in most romance novels, slowly. I know Jeremy knows I care about him, but I didn't realize how much until this moment.

"You don't have to be brave. You have to be smarter than they are. And you already are that and more. I'll talk to my dad about you staying here for the weekend. I'm sure he'd be fine with that."

Heat rises to my face. It's an uncomfortable sensation. My heart is in my lungs the way it does when a roller coaster dives. Jeremy has put me in a place I never thought I would be. I didn't want to have feelings for anyone in high school. I always imagined it would happen in college because mature relationships start in college.

This weekend, I'm going to need to brush these emotions aside with a broom. Sweep them under the rug until they go away. I know we've kissed before, and I'm not even sure why we did. Perhaps it was a validation kiss, one in which we both understood what we were going through as school rejects. But now we're on the other side, where I've fallen for Jeremy, and if the KAT trio indeed finds out, he's in trouble.

They know Jeremy and I are friends. They know we've kissed. But anyone can kiss for experimentation or curiosity. Maybe they have it on video. But they haven't heard me come out and say, *'Jeremy, I like you a lot.'* So, for me, the only way to keep Jeremy safe is to stop feeling.

Maybe staying in his house is a terrible idea. But what choice do I have when my bus-loving photo-snapping mother breathes air to humiliate me. I still haven't forgiven her for anything. I'm not ready to give her that.

Jeremy grabs my hand, and I let him. Our fingers twirl and slide together so easily there at his kitchen table. I want to look at his eyes and see their vastness. But I can't bring myself to find his eyes because it will make me blush if I do. If Jeremy sees me blush, he'll know that I've fallen for him.

"On second thought, maybe I shouldn't stay. I wouldn't want to make your dad angry or anything."

I pull away from Jeremy. If I pull away, will I remind him of his mom? Another woman who pulled out of his life. I'm scared of these feelings I'm having for him. My heart flutters like a moth trapped in a cage. If I keep the moth caged, it can't be free, but at least I know where it is at all times. Apart of me wants to turn around and release the moth. In that world, I'd kiss Jeremy over and over. He'd kiss my neck, and we'd date. But in this world, we are taunted by assholes who use the things we love against us.

And that's the last thing Jeremy needs, is for someone to hurt him. He doesn't need another reason to cut. He doesn't need another reason to die. Loving him would push him over the edge, and I can't let him jump. Because if he jumped, he'd be gone.

"What's up with you? You come to me for help. And now you're ditching me again? I can't keep up with you, Lily. Do you want to stay here or not?"

I know that whatever I say next will either make or break us. His black hair isn't covering his eyes like it does around everyone else. This is an outward sign of the trust he has in me.

"I want to stay. But I don't want you to get in trouble on my account," I reply.

I know the 'trouble' he thinks I'm referring to is with his dad for having a girl sleep here. But really, it's me not wanting him to get his ass kicked by the bullies at Asshole High.

"It will be fine. Hey, did you want to go to the zoo with me again? You don't have to help out this time."

I haven't looked at his eyes yet—the ones I want to see. However, I want to feel the moths jitter in their cage if I could feel that one more time, those moths inside would tell me that Jeremy Davis is alive and well.

"Sure, we can go to the zoo. What are we working on today," I ask?

"We won't be doing community service today. I was thinking more like we go to the zoo to have fun. They're open until eight."

"You mean just the two of us?"

"Is that a problem," Jeremy asks as his eyes find mine?

I've accidentally let my guard down, and Jeremy's found the keys to my caged moths. One moth escapes as I feel the redness find my cheeks. Jeremy puts his thumb on my right cheek dimple. It's like a puzzle. They fit so well together.

Like an idiot, I close my eyes, hoping Jeremy will kiss me. But, instead, he pulls my face towards his, and I feel his lips on mine. The world of ghouls doesn't exist. The bullies don't exist. All that exists is Jeremy.

He pulls away from the kiss, but I pull him in for more. Because I want him to know that somewhere in this world is a woman who is falling for Jeremy Davis, and that woman is me.

The Girlfriend

The doorknob turns, and Mr. Davis walks in. He looks the same as he did all those months ago at the pool.

"Jeremy, how was your day? My boss almost fired me. But I tell you, I've just about had it at that bank."

Mr. Davis doesn't notice me as he takes his trench coat off and hangs it on a hook. His large black shoes leave scuff marks on the floor.

"Dad, this is Lily."

Mr. Davis turns around, and a bright smile finds his face.

"Oh, well, excuse my manners. I remember you, Lily. You're that girl from the swimming pool. Sorry again that I didn't realize those girls were bullying you."

Jeremy turns to me like I'm supposed to report my bullying shenanigans to him.

"It's no big deal. I'll deal with them in due time," I say.

"Kids these days, they don't even have the guts to bully face to face. They do it through computers and cameras. Well, if those mean girls ever bother you again, you let me know," Mr. Davis says.

"What happened at the pool exactly," Jeremy asks?

The more we talk about the KAT trio, the further our worlds seem. I want to live in a world without ghouls who torment others for pleasure.

"The KAT trio ripped my book in half. They tossed me and the book in the pool. It's no big deal," I say, trying to shrug it off the way I always do.

"They are getting worse in their actions towards you," Jeremy comments.

"What happened now? Are those girls getting worse? Like I said, if you ever need help with those bitches, you let me know. I have connections with the school board."

Mr. Davis is willing to fight for me more than my parents ever have. I want to believe my parents mean well. But Mr. Davis was the first adult to witness my bullies attacking me. So he knows how they really are in action. My mother has only seen the aftermath.

"Thanks. The truth is they're the reason I am here now. They egged me and dumped flour on my head. So, I drove over here, and Jeremy let me take a shower. I hope that's okay," I say, as my eyes turn red.

"That's why you're in my son's clothes. I was wondering what was going on. Well, if there's anything I can do to help, let me know."

Mr. Davis is one of those super parents who exist to protect the weak. No wonder Jeremy feels safer with his dad than his mom.

"Actually, dad, there is something. Can Lily stay for the weekend? She had a falling out with her mom this afternoon."

"Oh, I see. Well, sure, stay as long as you'd like, Lily. You're more than welcome to have our guest bedroom."

A wave of excitement grows in my bones. Maybe life can be different, different in a good way. Maybe I am meant to live with Jeremy for a time. I've wanted to leave my parent's house for a while now. Living with Jeremy is the perfect opportunity to escape parents who didn't notice my pain.

"Thanks, Mr. Davis."

"There's no need to call me, Mr. Davis. Ben is fine."

"Thanks, Mr. Ben Davis," I say, as Mr. Davis and Jeremy laugh at my nervous response.

"You ready to go to the zoo," Jeremy asks?

"Oh, you're going out," Mr. Davis asks?

"Yeah, I'm taking Lily on a date. Is that okay?"

Jeremy says the word '*date*' so casually like we've been with each other for a long time. Are we together, and I didn't realize it? He hasn't asked me out yet or really indicated any real interest in me up till this point. Sure, he called me *pretty* before, but maybe it was to be polite. But now we are more than friends and less than dating. We are somewhere in between.

"Are you two dating then?"

Jeremy and I look at each other. No one replies to his question. I am dying to know the answer myself. Mr. Davis sees my face light up like red Christmas lights. It's obvious to him that I have feelings for his son.

"Well, whatever you are to each other, go have fun. Here's a twenty. The date is on me tonight."

"Thanks, Mr. Davis," I say as my voice cracks like a pubescent thirteen-year-old boy.

"You're welcome, and call me Ben."

Jeremy takes the money from his dad and grabs me by the hand. His dad stares at our hands and smiles. I'm not sure if that smile is him laughing inside at me, not wanting to call him 'Ben.' Or if, for the first time in forever, he is seeing his son happy with a girl. And that girl is me.

"Sorry about my dad. He gets excited when I have friends over."

When he says 'friends,' it kills the mood I'm in. One minute we are kissing and dating. And now I have been friend-zoned.

"Jeremy, what's going on between us? What am I to you? Are we friends? Are we...?"

I stop talking. Jeremy's hand finds its way into mine. The moths within my soul start dancing and throbbing around. He pulls into the zoo parking lot and doesn't seem anxious to get out.

"Listen, I like you...a lot. You're different from the other girls. I haven't dated lots of girls. But you, you seem to care...like you really want to be my friend. But then I see the way you look at me, and I haven't felt that since Melissa Brooke dumped me last year. She's from the next town over. She went to Dunlap High. She dumped me because she moved away. It really broke me when she dumped me. I understand why she did. But she never really seemed interested in asking questions about my life. I wanted her to ask or someone to ask. You seem like you want to ask me things. Are you ever going to?"

Jeremy's hand is sweaty from the shakiness of his voice. I hold it anyway because I know deep down somewhere within me that I love him. I don't know when it happened. Maybe it was when we met. Perhaps I fell for him at the zoo. But somewhere in all our interactions, I've fallen in love with Jeremy Davis. That scares the shit out of me.

"I... like...you, too. And I have wanted to ask you about the scars on your arms for a while now. I found the razors in the bathroom. I found the rubbing alcohol you use to clean the blades with. I was looking for shampoo, and I found them. I cried in the shower...when...I... found them. I don't want a... world without you...in it."

I can't have this conversation with Jeremy. It's too painful. A world without Jeremy is a world where he and I can't be safe. We keep each other safe.

I touch the scars on his arms and count them. Like the stripes of a tiger, they go all the way up to his shoulders on both arms. Some are deeper than others. They are like braille on his skin. Even a blind man could tell there is a story of pain that burns upon his epidermis. I touch his scars and feel them on his shoulders. These scars are everywhere on his body. Even his mid-section probably has scars everywhere. He has marked himself for life with these man-made scar tattoos.

"What good am I to this world, Lily? I've burned down a church. I embarrassed my dad at his workplace, to the point where he might get fired or leave. My mom and her abusive boyfriend won't leave me alone. The KAT trio and their boyfriends won't leave me alone. I was better off alone in that tree. You told me what they did to it. Now I have nowhere left to go. Want to know why I cut myself? Because living is harder than dying. I would be left alone if I was gone. No one would bother me or hit me. Does anyone care?"

The water streams down my face. He talks about dying like it's the only way out. But I can't let him leave me behind.

"I care, Jeremy. But please don't leave me here. You're the only friend I have."

The word *'friend'* triggers Jeremy. His eyes widen, and his clenched jaw relaxes.

"Friend? What does that word even mean? I haven't had a real friend since Melissa dumped me."

I'm not sure what Jeremy wants from me. I don't know what we are yet. If we are just friends, I can only hug him. If we're more, I can kiss him whenever I want.

"Jeremy, stop. We're friends. If you want to be, I'd even be your..."

Gosh! How I want to finish that sentence. How I want to fall in love with Jeremy with everything I am. But I'm scared of taking chances and taking the first step. But someone has to take action to save Jeremy from himself.

"I'd even be your girlfriend...if you'd want me to be. Because Jeremy..."

Jeremy Davis kisses me the way I've always wanted him to. With tears in his eyes, finding assurance in our new budding romance. We make out in his car and let the windows get foggy. And for once, I tune out the world and let myself enjoy him.

The Crickets of Vineyard Church

Our date to the zoo came and went. My mother blew up my phone while we were on our date.

Mom: Lily, please come home

Mom: Lily, where are you?

Mom: Lily, are you there?

I call mom to let her know where I'm staying. I haven't decided how long my stay with the Davis family will last.

"Mom, hi. I went to the zoo with Jeremy."

"You're with a friend? That's a relief. When will you be home? We need to get this bullying situation under control," mom says.

"I'll swing by later to get a few things. But I'm not staying at home. I need a few days to collect my thoughts. So, I'll be staying with the Davis family."

"The Davis family? Do you mean to tell me you're spending the night at that pyromaniac's house? He burned a church down, Lily-kins. No, you come home this instant. You stay away from that family," mom barks.

"I'm not coming home, mom. I'm eighteen, remember? So, I'm grabbing my clothes, and I'm leaving," I say. How does mom even know about the church burning? I must have said something in my sleep. I hate it when I sleep talk.

"Well, since you feel that way. Grab your things but don't bother coming home after that. After all, we've done for you, Lily-kins, this is how you repay us? By shacking up with that detention scum."

"His name is Jeremy, and he DID NOT burn the church down."

Jeremy stares at me while I am yelling at my mom on speakerphone. Finally, I hang up on her. I've had enough of our relationship to sink a ship.

"I take it you've just been kicked out of your house," Jeremy asks?

"Yeah, apparently. And she wants to help me with my bullying situation. Like kicking me out helps the situation. Can you swing by my parent's house? I need to grab my shit and get out."

Jeremy starts the car, and we hold hands. An understanding passes between us that we are more than friends. We are together. For a single moment on this car ride, I am happy.

Jeremy parks his car on the edge of the cul-de-sac and waits for me. I sneak into the house but am betrayed by the squeaky third step of the stairs.

"Lily, have you changed your mind and want to come home? But, first, we need to talk about the eggs and flour that were put on your face," mom says.

"I'm not ready to talk about it. I'm packing my bags, and I am leaving for a while. I need to clear my head."

I lock mom out of my room and start stuffing clothes, photos, and my favorite romance novels into a duffle bag. Mom kicks and hits the door like a crazy person. I open the window and sneak out from the back. I toss the duffle bag onto the ground and leap onto the backyard trampoline. Jeremy watches as I perform my daring circus act. I land on the trampoline and jump three times into the air. Mom yells at me through my bedroom window as I pick up the duffle bag.

"Don't you ever come back here...you ungrateful daughter."

Maybe I am ungrateful. But I need time. Time to process what the KAT trio has done to me. Time to think about what course of action to take next. Time to prepare for our next move.

"Where do you want to go next," Jeremy asks as the light of day begins to dim into the blackness of night?

"I want to go see the Vineyard Church."

"The Vineyard church, why?"

Jeremy drives a stick shift. I like watching him struggle to put the car into first gear. Then, I watch his foot tap the clutch.

"I want to look for evidence that you didn't do it. You might think the church burning down is your fault, but I know Kelly must have done and made it look like you did it all along. And if I am right, we might have a way at getting back at all of them."

Jeremy continues our drive into the night and parks the car in front of the remains of the Vineyard church. The wood still smells like fire. The ash and dust fly around in the air with the gust of wind. Burned Bibles and pews are scattered about in torn-up rows.

"I don't want to be here, Lily. This was a mistake. It's too painful."

"What's too painful? Tell me. I know you didn't do it. Kelly or her boyfriend made it look like you did," I tell him, to reassure him I know he's innocent.

"That's not it. I was here the night the church burned down. I drove over to the small town where Melissa, my ex, is from. She was visiting her friends for the weekend, and I wanted to see her one more time. She gave me some of my old belongings back and told me I was a fucked up suicidal mess. She told me to kill myself. Can you believe that the person I was in love with told me to die? So, I came here that night and lit up a cigarette to blow off some steam. I might have smoked five or six cigarettes. I don't really remember. Anyway, I was trying to talk to God or a higher power because I wanted to know if it was my time to clock out. Melissa knew I cut myself. It wasn't a secret. She never asked about it but always touched them. I was feeling ready for death that day. So, when no one stopped me from my thoughts, I decided to end my life that night. I found a rope in the church's janitor's office. It was long and sturdy when I pulled on it. I knew it was the noose meant for my neck. The church rafters had these high beams, right about here..." Jeremy says as he stretches to show the height of the beams with his hands.

I look up and imagine the familiar rafters he's referring to. I remember the beams. I used to stare at them and let my mind wander as the pastor spoke on Sundays. We didn't come to church often but occasionally did with my mom's friends.

"I knew I would hang nicely here. I was sick of being alive. My girlfriend abandoned me, and my mom fed me to her abusive boyfriend. The divorce broke me, and God himself didn't try to stop me from killing myself. I had the rope ready to go on my neck when Kelly walked into the church with Gerald. They had been following me that night. They used to stalk me from time to time. They laughed at me, called me a wimp, and pathetic for trying to clock out early. Gerald took the rope away from me, and Kelly took the cigarettes out of my pocket. She struck the match and lit a cigarette. She told me I deserved to burn in hell for choosing death. Instead, she wanted to help me get there faster. She dropped the cigarette next to me, and Gerald knocked me out. The next thing I knew, I was passed out with firefighters surrounding the church. I tried to tell them about Kelly and Gerald. But no one would believe it. They found nicotine in my system and found the lit cigarette next to me. The whole thing was blamed on me. Somewhere Gerald has that rope. I'm sure he's waiting for me to come back and get it. Maybe Kelly kept my cigarettes as a trophy. I will never know. Sometimes I think about that rope being around my neck. Maybe this world would have been better without me in it. But then I stop and think about you..."

Jeremy turns, and a twinkle in his eyes shows me a glimpse of happiness has returned to his life. Perhaps he can be saved after all.

"What about me? I've done nothing good for you."

Jeremy's hand finds mine in the dark beside the ruins of the old church.

"I know that's not true. You're always on a quest to save me. You're always pleading for my life. I know you're hiding something from me, and I want to know what it is?"

"Kelly threatened me and said she would hurt you if I didn't let her have her fun. Fine with me. So, I let her and her friends do what they like to me for an Instagram post. I was trying to protect you."

I turn around in fear that Kelly might have heard me confess the truth to Jeremy. There are no security cameras everywhere to spy on us. It's just Jeremy, me, and the night sky.

"Why would you want to protect me?"

It's then I decide to risk it all, to tell the truth, that's been bubbling inside me beside the caged moths.

"The...truth...the truth. I wanted to protect you because I love you, Jeremy. And a world without you in it is one I can't live in. You're my only friend, and if I have to get hurt to save your life, then that's what I'll do."

The autumn crickets chirp their last songs in the night air—an owl hoots as the creatures of night chatter among themselves.

Jeremy's hands are both in mine as his forehead rests against mine. Our lips are close to touching, as Jeremy whispers to me and me only, "I love you too, Lily Green."

Jeremy and I kiss beneath the star-dusted sky.

Eye of the Storm

Romance novels are the best medicine for the soul. I never knew I could be in my version of romance. But, this time, it's not a character in a book; it's me having a relationship with another person.

Jeremy breaks from our kiss and leads me to the car. The drive back is filled with handholding and Jeremy kissing the back of my hand several times. We don't say much to each other. Instead, we giggle and brush each other's hands together accidentally.

Mr. Davis is asleep in front of the tv when we get home. Jeremy puts a large comforter over his father. His glasses are still on his face. I slide them off, fold them down, and put them on a side table.

Jeremy carries my duffle bag into the guest bedroom. So, this is my home now for a while. I'll have to buy more clothes for myself later. Glad I have money from tutoring all those grade school kids.

I'm sure my mother will come to her senses and invite me home. A part of me hopes that's true. But I can't know for sure, can't know what parts are genuine and which parts aren't. So, my relationship with my mother is eggshells, and eggshells are the last thing I want to think about at a time like this.

The guest bedroom is small, plain, and ordinary. The bedsheets are light blue and match the light blue wallpaper. On the shelf is *The History of Pirates* book from Mr. Davis. I put it back in the Lending Library the day I got bullied. Jeremy must have found it and knew I put it in there.

"We could be like them, you know, "Jeremy says, pointing at the book on the shelf.

"Like who?"

"Like Anne Bonnie and Calico Jack, the pirates. They were in love and didn't let anyone hurt them."

I think about Jeremy as a pirate. He'd be a sexy pirate for Halloween or a costume party.

"Is that what we are? Is in love," I ask?

We both know the answer is yes because we shared a kiss at the ruins of the Vineyard Church.

Jeremy shuts the door behind him. I start to unpack my stuff. Jeremy helps me settle in.

"Are you going to be, okay? Staying here at my house," Jeremy asks? My question has still gone unanswered by him, should I be worried?

"It's not like I can go back home now. This year was supposed to be my year. I was supposed to volunteer and get good grades. Instead, my grades are all Cs and Bs. I've dropped out of all my volunteer jobs. I didn't tell you that. It was all piling on too much. I hope I can get into college."

"Why don't you go to the community college with me? They have an even bigger tree on campus for us to sit and make out in."

I hadn't considered the community college before. It would be cheaper, and with my current grades, it's the best chance I have right now.

"Maybe you can give me a tour of the campus sometime. I've never been there," I reply.

Jeremy sits beside me on the bed. A part of me is exhausted, and another part of me wonders if Jeremy will stay. Will he sleep next to me and hold me all night if he stays? Will he want to make love? Am I even ready for that?

My nervous system kicks into overdrive. I'm not sure I am ready for Jeremy to do all the things men do to women with their hands. But, on the other hand, if I turn him down, will he sink so far into depression that he'll end up hating me? Is being a girl this difficult? There are way too many thoughts in my head, tangled like a web.

Spider flight or ballooning is what spiders do to travel through the air. They build a web and let the air take them wherever they land. I was a spider in flight, and Jeremy caught my web and brought me home.

The problem with being a spider is at some point, I will need to feed. And feeding I plan to do when Kelly, Amy, and Tia least expect it. I know the truth now that Kelly has a potential pack of cigarettes hidden from the world. So, I need to set my trap and wait for her to fall into place.

"It's a great college. I'm going to study art. I want to be an art teacher someday."

It's nice to hear Jeremy talk about the future. It means he plans on living and staying with me, at least for a bit longer. Jeremy moves closer to me and leans me back on the bed.

"You'd be a good art teacher," I say again, trying to be calm and mature about how casual Jeremy seems to be about being on top of me.

I let him stay there for a while, and he rests his hand on my other one. Then, he pulls me closer to him and flips us over onto his back. I rest my head on his chest and listen to the sound of his heart beating. His chest rises and falls with his breath, and I know he's alive.

I kiss Jeremy on his bottom lip. It's the perfect place to kiss him. I nimble a little on it, and he puts his tongue in my mouth. I've read about French kissing and how passionate it can be and feel. All the things I've read are true. So just as quickly as he slides his tongue into my mouth, I do the same to him.

He puts me on my back and starts making out with me. It's all happening so fast that I don't have time to think. Do I want this? I don't have time to process. Is overthinking normal?

I'm eighteen. I'm old enough to have sex. Right now, everything is spinning. Spinning becomes a tornado, and tornados carry girls to wonderful places like Oz or another world beyond. The eye of the storm is the safest place to be. My life is a tornado, spinning like a top, constantly in motion. But Jeremy is the eye of the storm that I have found in the void. As the bullies have had their way with me, he's found me. As my mother kicks me out, he's found me.

He's always been there. Has always waited. This whole time I thought I was supposed to save Jeremy Davis. But this entire time, little by little, and day by day, it's me who's needed the saving. And Jeremy was the one to do it.

I lie on my back and break our kiss. Jeremy smiles, and I smile back as an assurance to let him know that I am ready to ride the upcoming storm. The eye of the storm won't last forever. But for now, we can enjoy its safety and worry about the consequences that tomorrow may bring. Jeremy and I make love on his bed, and it's better than all the love scenes I've read about in novels. I hope to write my own book someday, and when I do, I will tell the truth about how good sex really is.

Red and Blue Lights

The cop cars pull up to Jeremy's house early in the morning. The lights bounce around the room in a spinning red and blue haze. The sirens instantly wake us both up. This isn't the way I imagined waking the morning after sex. Jeremy's arms are wrapped tightly around my waist. It's still nice to know he stayed beside me, despite the cops being outside.

The doorbell rings, and the clock says that it's 6:40 in the morning—a knot forms in the pit of my stomach. I turn to Jeremy, who's as nervous as I am. We both know he's on probation for burning a church he didn't burn, creating a record that was never meant for him. The cops are the last thing he needs.

The cops ring the doorbell again. Mr. Davis gets up from the couch and turns the television off.

"Hello, who is it," Mr. Davis asks as he puts the sweatshirt on? He zips up the zipper halfway up his chest.

"The police, can we come in?"

Mr. Davis opens the door slowly. His eyes glow as they get bigger. Their wideness catches a glimpse of Jeremy and me standing and waiting at the top of the stairs. I fix my hair up and pull myself together.

"Sure, come inside, officers. What can we do for you this Saturday morning?"

Mr. Davis signals for both of us to come down the stairs. A part of me fears my mother and her craziness this morning. I wouldn't put it past her to call the police and claim I was kidnapped.

"We're investigating the murder of Gerald McLaren. We have reason to believe that your son, Jeremy, may have been involved."

Mr. Davis bites his lip as the hairs on my neck rise like the quills of a porcupine. Gerald McLaren is the asshole who is dating Kelly, the dumbass in the tutoring program. The idiot who threw eggs on me on Instagram.

"That's impossible. Jeremy's been with me this whole time," I say as Jeremy pulls my arm. He shakes his head. I know what that head shake means. It means that I need to shut up and let Mr. Davis take care of his son.

My eyes burn from the acid-like tears forming at the base of my eyelashes. My vision blurs as the tears appear. But, I don't let them shed. I don't let a single one trail down my face. I don't give my body the satisfaction of making me cry.

"And who are you," The officer with the name tag saying Reynolds asks?

"My name is Lily, Officer Reynolds," I reply.

"Are you Lily Green? The girl from the Instagram egging video that was posted yesterday?"

"Yes, why," I ask, knowing deep down I am somehow going to be blamed for being in the video?

"We are going to need you to come with us as well. There's a lot that happened last night. And it's our job to get to the bottom of this, Miss Green."

The blood in my soul boils almost to the point of boiling over. The KAT trio, primarily Kelly, is to blame for all of this. Kelly burned the church down and framed Jeremy.

"How do you know Jeremy was even there at his murder scene? When was Gerald murdered exactly," I ask?

I want to question all of their motives before they take Jeremy away. Jeremy shakes his head at me and just sits there. He sits there and takes their accusations like he's already committed a crime they can't prove yet.

"We have enough evidence that places Jeremy at the scene of the crime," Officer Reynolds says.

The other officer, whose name tag is missing, just stands there sipping his coffee like it is perfectly normal to wake people up before seven and accuse them of criminal injustice. His blonde hair fades into his eyes. I can't stand to look at either of them.

"What evidence," Mr. Davis asks?

Officer Reynolds pulls out pictures of the crime scene. The first photo they show us is of a pack of cigarettes, the same brand Jeremy has been known to smoke. A yellow box with the camel logo on the side. The second photo they reveal, I assume to be the murder weapon.

My heart throbs upon seeing the photos. It's like a great fist has sprung forth from a dark place and has squeezed my heart as tight as it will go. The blades are the same serrated blades that Jeremy has used to cut his body to pieces. If they take one look at his body, they will know he has been through a paper shredder. They will compare the blade marks, and it will all be over.

"Jeremy, are these your knives," Officer Reynolds asks?

Before Jeremy can speak, his dad pushes him down onto the couch.

"My son isn't saying anything until I get a lawyer."

"I understand your shock, Mr. Davis. He's entitled to a lawyer. It's within his legal rights. However, he still needs to come with us. He is our primary suspect. As for you, Miss Green, I think you should come quietly. We have a lot of questions to ask you down at the station."

My rib cage burns. My mouth becomes dry, and I can't form words in front of Officer Reynolds.

Jeremy Davis is anything but a murderer. He'd never hurt anyone but himself. I just know this misunderstanding will only jeopardize Jeremy's life even further.

Gerald McLaren was a basketball player. But he was also a dumbass. What if he had us all fooled? What if it was all an act, and he was never an idiot in the first place?

It's possible that Gerald was a bright and intelligent creature in some corner of the world. With Gerald dead, I'll never honestly know if Gerald or Kelly framed Jeremy about the church. I have a feeling that Kelly is the mastermind behind this whole thing, and since she was his girlfriend perhaps she murdered him and framed Jeremy. I've read enough books to know the lovers are usually the first to be overlooked, and they always end up being the murderer. Who's to say it's not the case here?

Officer Reynolds lets Jeremy and me change into more comfortable clothes. He takes Jeremy's clothes and puts them into an evidence bag like it will prove anything. If Jeremy murdered Gerald, I would have noticed.

Gerald was alive after school throwing eggs and laughing at me on an Instagram live video. I drove straight to Jeremy's house after that. We went to the zoo and made love in his house. When would Jeremy have had time to murder Gerald?

Before we follow Officer Reynolds and the unknown police officer out of the door, Mr. Davis stops them.

"Can I see the picture of the murder victim? I want to look at it before you leave."

Officer Reynolds digs around in the vanilla folder and hands it to Mr. Davis. I catch a quick glimpse, and it's enough to make me vomit. Five stabs are in his midsection. Gerald McLaren's blood surrounded his body on all sides of that picture. And all the while, I'm haunted by how these events will haunt Jeremy and me. But mostly, I fear that the events of this morning will be the reason Jeremy Davis will actually commit suicide.

Interrogation

Sweat and urine are the two smells stinking up the back of the police car. Sitting in other people's bodily fluids is enough to make me want to heave. Jeremy's hands are cuffed in the car. He stares out the window and watches the trees wave at him in the morning sun. It might be the last time Jeremy Davis sees the sun for a long time.

Pretty soon, they will take Jeremy away and hide him forever. There's too much evidence that puts him at the crime scene. Even if I told them everything about Jeremy and where he was last night, I am not convinced they'd fully believe me.

It's not fair that Kelly planted the cigarettes. I'm not sure when Kelly got a hold of Jeremy's knives. My guess is she snuck into the Davis' house and looked around for something. I'm not sure when she broke in. Did she do it months prior? How long was she watching Jeremy Davis? Maybe the knife isn't even his. It could all just be a big misunderstanding.

The police car pulls into the station. Before he gets out of the car, I kiss Jeremy on the lips. My eyes tell him that I love him. His black hair falls in front of his eyes, and that's how I know he isn't okay.

If noticed by anyone, his hair tells a story of pain and shyness. When his hair falls over half his face, he keeps them all out. But for me, I've seen his whole face. His hair has moved to the side so that I can see both of his eyes. I've seen his smile light up from ear to ear, and that's how I know he loves me. He revealed his whole self to me. But now, as his hair falls over his face and they take him away. The happiness we've shared will end, and my boyfriend will be gone, quite possibly forever.

The photos of the knife victim, Gerald McLaren, flood my mind. The five stab wounds in his midsection become too real, too powerful like a nightmare burning into my flesh. I can feel all of them—all the wounds and sores that Gerald suffered. I hurt where all the pain inside of me dwells. My stomach hurts in five locations, like Gerald's stab wounds. Five tight knots and five more caged moths.

"Okay, Miss Green, come with us. We have a lot of questions to ask you. So please follow us this way," Officer Reynolds says like any of this is normal.

I might have been more willing to have a normal conversation with him if Officer Reynolds let us be comfortable at the Davis' house. But instead, I have to feel intimidated and ripped away from any comfortable environment. Metal chairs and hard plastic tables. A room with no pictures, just four white walls, and nothing to stare at. Nothing to distract my thoughts.

No matter what they ask me or how they ask me. I know the truth. That Jeremy Davis never killed Gerald McLaren. Maybe he killed himself, which is unlikely due to the stab wounds. Whoever it was had to be close to him, more intimate than anyone. Someone like Kelly. Or someone else that has been looked over.

The room I sit in is as dull as I imagined it to be, with a few things to look at—a black window at my side and clear on the other side for whoever is watching my conversation. I was never handcuffed. I assume I am a free woman until I say something they don't like. Then maybe, just maybe, I will be sporting a new pair of handcuffs.

"Miss Green, before we begin, do you know why we have called you here today?" Officer Reynolds asks while pouring me a cup of coffee. I take the coffee. I could use some caffeine to calm the nerves that these cops have triggered.

"Honestly, Officer Reynolds, with how the last twenty-four hours have played out, nothing surprises me anymore."

I'm pretty sure the answer I just gave them was not a typical response. But what else is new? I cannot say a proper thing in a normal social environment. So how is this any different from that?

"Oh, and why is that?"

"You tell me, Officer. Why am I here," I ask, repeating his original question back at him?

"You're here. Not because you are in trouble, but because we saw the video on Instagram."

Officer Reynolds pulls out the dreaded egg and flour video for me to see. It's like I am being mocked. Regardless of deleting my account, this video will follow me to every job interview I apply to. In addition, this video will be archived with the rest of my shame videos and pictures.

"What about the video," I ask, wondering where he is taking this conversation? I want to break Jeremy out of here and live in a forest cabin with wood elves.

"Miss Green, is this you in the video? Are you the person being egged and having flour dumped on their head?"

"Yes, that's me. I would prefer not to watch that video. Put that away, please. It was humiliating enough."

My face gets flushed. Thinking about getting bullying makes me mad.

"And who egged you? "

"The KAT Trio, Kelly, Amy, and Tia. And then Kelly's boyfriend was there. Gerald McLaren was her boyfriend. He's the deep voice you hear laughing in the background."

I hope Officer Reynolds isn't suggesting I have something to do with the murder of Gerald McLaren.

"Has Gerald McLaren bullied you for a long time?"

"No, that was the first time he was ever involved. I usually get bullied by Kelly. If you should interview anyone, it should be her."

I take a sip of coffee. It's the worse tasting coffee I've ever had. It takes like Pepto Bismal made love to a pile of dirt. But I keep smiling and pretend to enjoy it.

"Tell me more about Kelly."

Officer Reynolds looks at the security camera and then back at me.

"She was out to get me. Before school started, she ganged up on me at a swimming pool. Her group pushed me into a pool and ripped my favorite book in half. She also has said and done embarrassing things to me on social media. I deleted my account to avoid the harassment."

"What do you know about Jeremy Davis," Officer Reynold asks while taking a sip of his coffee?

"He likes to be alone. He used to sit in the big tree at Harris Park. He seems a bit depressed to me."

"Why do you say that?"

"His parents got into a divorce. He mentioned not being happy about that."

"What's your relationship to Mr. Davis? Are you romantically involved?"

Officer Reynolds's circle of questions makes my head spin on its axis. He's looking for something, a flaw, or a motive. I am trying to keep Jeremy intact because I don't want to see him die.

"I would say we are on our way to dating."

"Have you had sex? Did Mr. Davis force himself on you?"

"What no? Why are you asking me that? I love Jeremy."

I've spilled my heart out. Now I will be known as the girlfriend of a suspected murderer.

"Where were you after the egg incident after school yesterday?"

"I went to Jeremy's house to get away from my mom. Then I went to my parent's house to pack up some clothes. After that, I was invited to stay with the Davis family for a while. We went on a date and went back to his house. We ended up having sex and fell asleep. Next thing I know, you knocked on the door this morning, and here we are having this lovely conversation now."

"How long has Jeremy been cutting himself?"

My eyes widen at the thought of Jeremy carving into himself, let alone another person.

Officer Reynolds slams another photo of Gerald McLaren's body on the table. The five stab wounds call my name. I can't look at it. It's so awful. Gerald McLaren was an idiot. Gerald McLaren was my student. I tutored him for a season, and now he is dead in a photo before my eyes.

Next, Officer Reynolds pulls out the murder weapon and shows it to me. To my horror, the weapon has familiar initials carved into the side of it 'J.D.' At this moment, I'm questioning everything important to me. What if Jeremy Davis did kill Gerald McLaren? Who's to say he wouldn't come after me? I am not sure I can trust everything I know about Jeremy Davis for the first time.

Three Little Notes

Officer Reynolds lets me leave the police station, but not Jeremy. Since Jeremy isn't around, Mr. Davis has asked me to leave his house; he thinks having me around is inappropriate. The last place I want to go to is my mom's house. There's too much drama to my name now, and I can't have it affect my dad.

As I leave the Davis' house, I decide to do a little investigative research on Jeremy by myself. The Lending Library calls me to its doors. The little post sits like a mailbox on the edge of the street. I open the doors and find three letters inside, all with the initials J.D.

Dear Lily,

I didn't want to give this letter to you. Letters are the only way I can talk to you. They are the only way I can get my thoughts out. I want to tell you the truth. I'm writing this to you while you're sleeping. You fell asleep quickly after we had sex. But I had to tell you the truth, that Gerald McLaren is dead.

I had no part in it. After you fell asleep, I snuck out to confront the KAT trio. Amy and Tia held a gun to my head. I wanted to tell them all to leave you alone. But they wouldn't listen. So instead, they searched my pockets and found my favorite pocketknife. It has my initials 'J. D' on the side.

I'm writing this to you in case something terrible happens to me. Kelly is the true villain. She murdered her boyfriend with my pocket knife. He was the only one to agree with me that they took their bullying with you too far. He wanted to apologize to you, Lily. But Kelly, she wouldn't listen.

She took the gun from Amy and held it to my head. She said she would shoot me if I didn't hurt Gerald for agreeing with me. She fired three rounds into the air to let me know she was telling the truth. I picked up that knife and dropped it to the ground. Instead, Amy and Tia hit Gerald with a large rock and knocked him out. Kelly stabbed Gerald in the chest five times while lying in his cold blood. I barely got away. I didn't bother to get my knife. I know it condemns me to prison. But I had to get away, to see you one last time before the KAT trio got away with it.

The last thing I saw was Kelly throwing cigarettes next to Gerald's body. They must have been the ones she took from me the night the Vineyard church burned to the ground. I know I am going to be in trouble for this before the cops arrive. But please, Lily, know that I love you. Please believe me.

-J. D

The two other notes rest between my shaking hands. Jeremy knew he would get in trouble for the murder he witnessed last night. Why didn't he tell me this morning? Why didn't he say anything to the cops? He said nothing this morning. So now he will be blamed for a crime he didn't commit. Can I turn this note in for evidence? Why did he leave this note in the Lending Library? Am I really that predictable? Did he really know I was going to come back here to look for clues?

The other two notes shake me to my core. The notes aren't in Jeremy's handwriting; it's Kelly's handwriting. It looks like hers anyway. It's the same bubbly large print I recognize from our years of forced homework partnership.

The first potential Kelly written note is a drawing of the Vineyard church. It appears to be a floor plan, with' *Revenge on Jeremy'* written in blue pen. Tears stream down my face.

The vomit comes to my throat. The acid burns my tongue as it forces its way out. There goes the morning coffee I had at the police station. This whole time it really was the KAT trio. My head spins up and down. I hear a ringing in my ears.

The second note is crinkled in my left palm. Do I dare open this note?

The second note is a drawing of the big tree in Harris Park. Again, there are drawings of stick people with names above their heads. It's a picture of Kelly's master plan to egg me, destroy Jeremy's tree, and ruin our relationship.

On top of this second note in blue pen, it reads, "Revenge on Lily Green." From the time I was five until now, I have feared Kelly. I don't know how Jeremy got these notes from Kelly. But it's clear to me from this handwriting that it's all Kelly. Tia and Amy have had their part to play in her little game. But it's time for someone to challenge who she is and what she represents, a bully—a bully to her core.

She may have won the small battles, but framing Jeremy for a murder he didn't commit crosses too many lines. It crosses all the lines. When you cross all the lines with me and push a victim over the edge enough, you'd better watch your own back. Kelly Elizabeth Butterfield, I am coming for you, and this time I am ready to fight and defend Jeremy's honor.

Did He Do It?

By the time I get home, I don't even remember why I was mad at my mother in the first place. Something about bullying and the KAT trio: whatever the reason, my egg situation is nothing compared to Jeremy getting framed.

The tv is playing softly in the background as I sneak in through the back door. The news is playing, and all over the news, to my horror, is Jeremy Davis. His mug shots, the photos of Gerald McLaren's corpse mangled and defiled on television. But, of course, I wasn't Gerald's friend, only his tutor. But if Jeremy told me in a letter that Gerald wanted to apologize to me for egging me, and that's why Kelly tried to kill him, then I believe Jeremy. I believe Jeremy right down to my bones.

Photos of the murder weapon are shown on the news. I walk past my parents, and like a fly attracted to light, I can't bring myself to pull away. My parents are talking, but it's white noise. I can barely understand the English being broadcasted to me on the screen. Not sure if my parents know what I know. Or have seen what I have seen.

The cops wanted to contact my parents while I was at the station. Being of legal age, I declined at the time. So that's me trying to prove to my parents that I can handle myself. That their precious little Lily-kins doesn't need to be babysat. But right now, I need a dad to give me a hug and a mom to make me soup. Because Jeremy, my love, is going to die.

He won't die by their hands. He will die on his own in a prison cell. If anyone is going to kill Jeremy Davis, it will be his own worst enemy, his inner demons. The note he wrote me is the same handwriting from the day he was jotting down notes in his journal in the big tree.

More images flood the screen. My eyes grow heavy watching the news and my personal life being broadcasted. The video of the KAT trio egging me features next. I am the highlight for the Sunday evening news. Already this weekend has been a big mishap that I have had the misfortune of knowing.

My eyes cry as my mother shuts the tv off. The last thing I see on the screen is my face covered in flour with the caption reading "*Is Bullying on the Rise at Ashmore High*?" Well, no shit, it is. It has been there from the dawn of time. Anyone who knows the school library, as well as I do, would know that yearbooks are evidence of the year-to-year mockery predating back to the Great War, *World War II*. There are photos defiled with comments like "Go to hell and die."

I go to my room and shut the door. I don't want my parents to see me cry over Jeremy Davis. My yearbook sits in the back of my bedroom closet, collecting dust. I search for Jeremy's picture and find the photo of the boy with the familiar hair on his face. Below his name is the quote he chose to have written in the yearbook last year, *"I hope to live a life that people remember. I only hope I live to see that day."*

It's as clear as day to me that Jeremy was planning to kill himself even then. He just needed a motive. He just needed a reason to stop breathing.

I think back to the conversation Jeremy and I had the night we made love for the first and only time.

"We could be like them, you know,"Jeremy says.

"Like who?" I ask.

"Like Anne Bonnie and Calico Jack, the pirates. They were in love and didn't let anyone hurt them."

But we aren't like them. We are forever twisted like the victims that we are. We can't protect ourselves, and I couldn't protect you, Jeremy. What can I do? What should I do?

"Lily, let me in. We need to talk."

I open the door for my mom. I let her in for the first time in days. I cry about getting egged. I ball for Jeremy and the life they think he's living.

"Lily, did Jeremy kill that boy?"

I can't form words. All I can do is hand my mother the letter. I watch her eyes scan the document. Her eyes frantically read from left to right. As she is reading the letter, I can tell that her eyes have gone from blaming Jeremy Davis to believing every word he has written. Finally, as our eyes meet, I can tell that my mother will quit her bullshit and help me the way a real grown-up should. The kid in me takes her by her hands and pulls her in for the biggest hug.

The Cleaning Tree

The following two weeks are silent. My patience was being tested. My emotions are like a landmine, waiting to go off. If Kelly crosses my path, I hope she steps on the landmine and hears my verbal explosion. It's about time someone told Kelly the truth that she is mean, cruel, and heartless.

I set up a new Instagram account. In doing so, I will do some digging on Kelly with my new username and alias. My fake name is *Jennifer Smith*. It's a generic enough name that I could be anyone. My profile picture is of an orange tabby cat wearing glasses—a fat Garfield-like cat, sitting on a large book. Maybe the book is a dead giveaway that it is really me.

My computer mouse gets stuck, and I am forced to use the lousy touch mouse on the keyboard. As I scroll through Instagram, as 'Jennifer,' I see the truth on Kelly's profile. She has photos of Gerald McLaren with a before picture of them together and an after picture of his death. Both are next to each other. I screenshot my laptop screen. This evidence might help me save Jeremy.

My Instagram account receives an instant private message. I open it up, and it's from Kelly. I know from her end; she will read the 'just seen' message that appears. It's an indicator that the other person is present and watching the message now.

Kelly: Hello, Train Tracks.

My heart pounds. How does she know this dumb alias is me?

Me: Hello, do I know you?

I pretend to be someone else.

Kelly: It's obviously you. You have a book in your profile picture. It's the picture you use for your bookmark. I remember that picture. That bookmark was in your copy of *The Kissing Booth*. I took the bookmark out before I tossed your copy into the pool. Do you remember?

I screenshot this conversation as it takes place. Maybe I can get her to confess in the chatroom. I decide to let her taunt me over the PM. If I let her have her bullying fun, it might be enough to help Jeremy.

Me: You caught me. What do you want?

Kelly: Did you see those pictures of Gerald? Poor thing. I can't believe your boyfriend killed mine.

Me: I can't believe you killed your boyfriend for wanting to apologize to me.

Kelly: It sure was fun. Watching him die.

Me: So, you killed Gerald?

Kelly: No. Jeremy did that. I only smiled and watched.

Me: You killed Gerald.

Kelly: You can't prove it, Lily-kins. Did you really think I'd confess in a PM?

Me: I know what you did, and you will pay.

Kelly: Bye, Train Tracks. And don't forget to do my paper about the Salem Witch Trials. It's due in a week. Or else something bad might happen to your parents.

Kelly slipped up without realizing it. I screenshot the message. Her threat to my parents won't go unnoticed by a cop. Now the ball is in my court. I can either use my parents as bait or turn her in now. Apart of me wants to see how far Kelly will take this. I know she wouldn't kill my parents because I am onto her, and she knows it. But she will do something, and I need to be a few steps ahead of her.

It works in my favor that I didn't show my mother the other two notes of Kelly's master plans. Those notes are evidence against Kelly and now this private message. I screenshot the conversation. I copy and paste it into a document and print it. I put all of my spy work in a file under my bed. If I am going to be smart, I need to beat Kelly.

I skip school on Monday. It's been two weeks since Jeremy was taken away, and the cops interviewed me. I've avoided the KAT Trio. However, the tree in Harris Park still needs attention, and before Jeremy gets out of jail, like I hope he will, I need to clean the tree for him. The tree is his sacred space, his holy perch.

Geoffrey Chaucer is who Jeremy used to remind me of. He would observe the world. Did he watch the KAT trio and anticipate their horrible moves from his perch? Did he observe them from an alias on Instagram?

I park my mom's car in front of the Harris Park tree and find some remaining eggshells. There are a few remaining eggshell fragments from my humiliation. I throw them in a trash bag. I scrub the tree and get some of the spray paint off. I work for hours. The sweat comes to my pores. It takes me six hours to clean the big tree. I put a new rope ladder on the nails of the tree. I climb up and sit as Jeremy would.

My favorite book keeps me company. *The Kissing Booth* keeps my mind off my reality. Hopefully, Jeremy will let himself live a little longer so he can see justice being served on his behalf.

Mr. Davis

"Lily-kins, are you ready to go?"

My mother wakes me up. I don't know what day it is. I can barely remember my own name. It's been an exhausting turn of events. Seeking revenge on my bully is not something I ever thought I would do or could do. I can definitely not discuss my revenge plans with my mom. I could talk about this with a best friend in another life if I had one of those. But there will be plenty of time for that in college. If I can take a bully down, I will know I am prepared for college and being on my own.

"Ready for what, mom? Can't this wait? I am exhausted. I don't want to go anywhere."

"For your braces. Today you are getting them off," mom replies.

My mother forgot to tell me about the single most important day of my entire youth. It would have been nice to have this day carved in stone as a holiday. My own personal Memorial Day to commemorate that I no longer have to bear the name of *Train Tracks*. No more *Caged-Face* either. No more *Metal Mouth*. All their names can bite me before I bite them with my brace-less grin.

I take out my phone and begin to text Jeremy. But unfortunately, my excitement is overshadowed by the fact that he is still very much in jail. Disappointment clings to my face as a frog clings to his lily pad.

"Oh, honey, were you about to text Jeremy?"

I nod and shake a little. All of my feelings hold my breath back.

"Mom, it's so not fair. I know you believe me when I say he didn't do it. I know you read the letter. I just want him to be out of that place. I picture him in there with his anxiety and his thoughts. I don't want him to die, mom. Did you know he was suicidal? He has wanted to die several times. But then I came into his life. I made him happy. He was finally getting out of his shell. But then all of this murder shit happened. I hate that he's in there."

Apart of me wants to tell my mom the truth. That revenge is coming for Kelly. But she doesn't need to get involved in that. The last time she tried, I ran away from her. I ran away from my mother and her attempts at bullying wisdom. Because I am eighteen now, and any comfort she has for me on bullying is too little too late.

"I do believe Jeremy. We just have to trust the system. It will work. It always does."

That's my mother's way of saying that they've never put an innocent man behind bars. Jeremy is eighteen, just like I am. He would be placed in an adult prison. He might get beaten up in there or worse. He might even take his own life knowing that living behind bars isn't worth it for someone like him. Even if they allowed him to take a college degree inmate program, he wouldn't do it. He'd choose death, or death would pick him. They are tethered forever. Jeremy flirts with death in an endless tango that I will never understand.

"Whatever you say, mom. Let's get these darn things out of my mouth now."

I needed to change the subject. Talking about Jeremy makes his absence surface.

"Mom, can we have Mr. Davis over for dinner? I think Jeremy would like to know his father is being looked after."

Mom smiles, and I see her pearly white teeth. Her teeth are smooth and don't have any silver braces on them. I can't wait to get these out of my mouth. They poke my teeth and tear my mouth to shreds from my top teeth to my bottom ones.

"Sure, honey, we can have Mr. Davis over for dinner. Get in the car. Your appointment starts soon."

My appointment is not a lengthy endeavor. My orthodontist wears his gloves and smiles at me from behind his medical mask. His gloves enter my mouth, and I hear buzzing sounds. Things pop, and screws loosen. The top braces are placed on a tray before me, and the bottom ones follow. For the first time in six years, I can glide my tongue across my top and bottom teeth and not feel a metal sensation upon them.

He hands me a mirror, and I see my teeth. My natural smile is the only one that doesn't crack mirrors—the reflection of someone who is no longer Train Tracks.

"I'm sorry that your boyfriend isn't here to see you without braces. I heard about that boyfriend of yours. I'm sorry he was a bad egg. Speaking of eggs, I am sorry that the egging video got out in the first place. I made my daughter delete her Instagram account after she kept watching it repeatedly."

Dr. Iggy means well. But with the last name like that, no wonder he can't mind his own business.

"Thanks, Dr. Iggy. My boyfriend didn't do it. You'll see. Thanks for taking my braces off."

I walk into the waiting room, and for once, I let my mother take a picture of me without my braces on. My life is a photo album. My parents have a child photo shrine descending and ascending the wall of our stairs. All of my baby photos and grade school photos are lined up with every step going up those stairs.

I drive my mother home and borrow the car to go to the Davis' house. It's hard to walk up the Davis' front porch steps. Finally, the doorbell chimes, and Mr. Davis or Ben, as he'd prefer, I call him, walks up to the door.

"Hi, Lily, what a surprise. How can I help you? Jeremy isn't here..." He trails off. We both know where Jeremy is, in jail, rotting away with his suicidal thoughts.

"I was wondering if you'd like to have dinner with my family tonight. We don't want you to be alone. So, we're ordering pizza and aren't doing anything fancy," I reply.

"Sure, that would be nice. I'm sorry Jeremy isn't here..." He looks down with sad eyes.

"He didn't do it, Mr. Davis. And one way or another, I will prove his innocence."

"You don't have to do anything, Lily. But thanks for the thought."

I take Mr. Davis to our house, and I see him light up for an evening. He smiles just like Jeremy and has older eyes that look like Jeremy's. However, there is one significant difference, Mr. Davis's eyes aren't full of suicidal thoughts. They are instead full of fear. Fear for the son we both know could take his own life if too much time passes by.

Bait

Worms are smooth and wiggly creatures. Birds love to eat them, and their pink heads look like their pink bottoms. They are slimy creatures that are great to use when one goes fishing. A fisherman takes his hook and pierces the side of the worm on the end of a fishing pole. The fisherman casts his line into the river and waits.

That's what I've been doing with my parents. I've been like the fisherman. I've prepared my parents as bait for Kelly. After a while, a fish will see the wiggling worm and attack the bait. I can only hope that Kelly will go for the bait. Accept this time; it will be like me springing the trap and bringing her to justice. If I could get her to confess, to really confess to the murder of Gerald McLaren, then the world would be a much better place.

Fishermen wait for hours to catch their fish. Fish are bullies who eat to survive. They go into the bellies of fishermen and never come out. This is where I am now, waiting in the river—hoping and waiting for that fish to swim upstream. If I stay long enough, the bully fish will appear, and justice can be served for Gerald McLaren and Jeremy Davis.

Maybe I sound like a whiny vengeful girlfriend, but I don't think so. The congregation of the Vineyard church deserves to know the truth about what really happened the night their beloved house of God went up in flames.

If I plan like Kelly and draw out my plans, maybe I can see the way she sees. Study the way the mind of my bully works. I take out my notebook, the one I was given in middle school with the fuzzy hot pink cover. I draw a big circle at the center of the first empty page and write 'Big Tree at Harris Park.' It's the perfect location to trap Kelly.

The KAT trio has been known to attend the weekend outside Yoga classes. If my family could attend this class, it would annoy Kelly. But, getting under her skin is exactly what I need to do if I can save Jeremy Davis from killing himself in prison.

I bet he feels hopeless in there and exposed to a lie that isn't his truth. So, he wears that crime like it's his crown of thorns to wear. But it's not for him to wear and not for him to bear their crime.

I quickly go online and see the advertisement I was hoping to find. The Saturday Lawn Lover's Society is hosting their Yoga class this Saturday by the Big Tree in Harris Park. It's at eleven in the morning, and we can have a picnic in the clean tree that I have prepared for Jeremy. I head downstairs with my phone in my hand. I'm prepared to hand my mother my phone and show her my supposed brilliant idea for family bonding and relaxation.

"Mom, I think we should all do Yoga in the park this Saturday."

My mother looks up from her obvious erotic novel. By now, her book characters are having sex and are getting down and dirty. I know what sex readers' eyes look like. I've had that guilty turned-on face before. There's no time to discuss my mother and her soft porn reading addiction.

It's no secret that my parents have stopped sleeping in the same room at some point in middle school. I'm convinced they stayed together for me and me alone. When I go to college, their relationship will diminish, and someone will leave. They live separate lives and sleep like an 18th century married couple in two separate bedrooms. My mom sleeps in the guest bedroom. The pillows are made of foam and are suitable for migraines.

"Why do you want to do yoga? Do you think it will help you relax or something? We aren't Jedis."

"Mom, *Star Wars* isn't real. Yoga might help me recover from my egg trauma, and it's in Harris Park. I haven't been to that park since that day. The day they egged me."

I know I am creating a slight fabrication to make up for the truth that I need to seek peaceful yoga revenge on the KAT trio. They will be there with their Yoga mats and will take deep breaths. I plan to be rude and distracting. At the very least, it will let Kelly know that she hasn't won. Not really.

"Sure, we can all go if you think it would help you heal. Are you sure you're ready for this? I know that boy of yours lived in that tree."

I think of Jeremy and the slim chance I have at ever kissing his lips again. Those sweet tender lips that have only loved mine. Besides his first love, he would use to make me jealous on occasion.

"Can we maybe have a picnic under the tree? I miss Jeremy, and it would be nice to be reminded of him a little after we do yoga in the park."

My mother agrees and takes me to a hippy yoga store called *Guru for You*. By the name of this store, I expect the manager to be a real Jedi Master. The force is present in this building if it is real at all.

A slender older woman with a patch over her eye comes and greets my mother. The room smells like incense, and it burns a part of my soul that I didn't even know needed to burn. The rest of the room is like getting high on cinnamon sticks and ginger root. The air is so thick I swallow it with my exhale.

"Where are your yoga mats," my mother asks as she's playing with a tub of lucky rabbit's feet? I urge my mother to buy one. I don't believe in luck, but I can use all the silly help I can get with Jeremy's life on the line.

"Over there by my cat," the odd elderly witch-like woman says as her eye patch snaps from her adjustment of it.

The lady points at a freak show cat with a drooping pink nose and two empty eye sockets. My goosebumps have made their way to my pores and not in a good way. This *Guru for You* store is where people get kidnapped in my nightmares.

The yoga mats stink. I grab two blue ones and pay the pirate wench elder as quickly as possible. The demon cat stretches and yawns. It purrs and hisses almost simultaneously, like two evil voices having a battling duet.

Before Saturday, the yoga mats have been bleached and left to dry in my bathroom. Dad reluctantly goes to yoga class with us. He claims his body isn't what it used to be. For a former diver in high school, he sure lost all flexibility in college. He only saved his flexibility for when he made me with mom. They haven't touched each other since.

The Harris Park is filled with eager yoga students. I sign my family up and pay the student fee for everyone. We fill out forms asking how flexible we are. I put that we can't touch our kneecaps on the slip. This should be painful at best. I fake my newfound love of yoga for my parents. They are there to be the bait. Like Kelly would do anything to them with other people present. This is the perfect plan and the only way to know if my parents are in real danger. The kind of danger that murdered Gerald McLaren.

After filling out waivers and the promise of an *I Won't Sue You* form, we make our way to the yoga class lawn spot. There are at least thirty students. The KAT trio arrives with their matching pink outfits like delusional barbie dolls. Kelly's eyes find mine, and all the confidence I built in my head evaporates.

The trauma of reading the letters floods my mind. The images of Gerald's body return. The chills of reading those creep scam letters surface. It all surfaces, but then my tongue glides on my teeth. And her power to call me Train Tracks is gone, and my confidence returns.

The KAT trio sets up their yoga mats two rows away from my parents and me.

"It's time to take our first deep breath class. We have some new faces. Welcome! Stretch your arms slowly and do what I do."

We breathe and stretch to the count of three. I make a loud snort sound. Kelly opens her eyes. Another deep breath and I burp loudly. My mother thinks I am sick to my stomach from the trauma. After a few more snorts and burps, Kelly's hatred surfaces.

"Knock it off, Train Tracks."

I smile widely to show Kelly my lack of braces. Her jaw clenches in all the right places. The class ends, and my legs hurt from the waist down. Dad stopped halfway through and drank his water.

After the class leaves, Kelly hangs around. She eyes my parents. My parents don't know who Kelly is. They don't know what she's done, and they certainly wouldn't recognize her voice from my egging video.

We spread a blanket out for our picnic in front of the big tree. After ten minutes of eating our lunch, I notice Kelly has gone. Dad goes to the car to rest his legs and drink water. Yoga was not a good healthy activity for dad. I head to our cooler to get a soda. I could use a Coke today. While dad is in the car, mom lets out a scream. Somewhere between dad going to the car and me getting a soda, Kelly perched in the big tree. She sits on the throne that is rightfully Jeremy's. The scream mom lets out is due to a knife that has stabbed her back. Dad doesn't know what's going on, but I do.

All the people have left the park. There are no witnesses or security cameras to capture Kelly's bitterness. Sometimes bait wiggles, and the fish doesn't fall for it. When the worm lets its guard down, the bully fish strikes. When the bully fish strikes, the fight to the death is over.

Kelly stabs my mother three times in the chest and back in broad daylight. All I can do is cry and run to the tree from the blue cooler. The world slows down as Kelly runs away. Dad gets out of the car as mom falls to the ground. My mother closes her eyes as blood surrounds the picnic blanket beneath the big tree in Harris Park.

Scarlett Death

My mother is dead. Her blood stains surround the base of the big tree. The big tree that once held my boyfriend in its branches now cradles my dead mother at its base.

I'm in shock, and it feels like horrifying shivers going through my nervous system. Kelly has won. She's taken my mother from me. I always knew that my mother and I didn't get along. I always assumed we would have more time to apologize and understand each other. More time to become best friends in my post-college years when I would be married and have three kids. She would have been a wonderful grandma, but that future is no more.

A future I thought I would have is ripped away from me within thirty seconds. I place my mother's head on my lap and let her blood drip all around me. I soak in this last moment I will ever have her beside me.

My body has been shivering for five straight minutes. My head is spinning and asking questions like, *why did she have to be murdered in a park?* My father will never forgive me once he finds out that I used them both as live bait.

Her blood still pours out and drips down the side. I take my hand and close her eyelashes. Her eyes are tender, and her breath is no more. My forty-eight-year-old mother is no more. I shut her mouth as the shock of it all sinks in.

My father runs over from the car. The world has stopped spinning. The love of his life is dead. Yet, despite them sleeping in separate rooms, it is clear from this moment that he always cared about her. He always loved her, and now the healing and counseling they could have used to save their marriage has been stripped away by Father time. I know what it feels like to have my love taken away from me.

My dad wails, and I step aside. I put my mother's head down on the ground. Then, as I turn around, my father begs Father time to rewind back to thirty minutes ago when we were all happy and eating our picnic food.

The picnic blanket is still nearby, and out of respect for my mother, I hand it to my father to wrap her in. A nearby man calls 9-1-1. He yells at the woman on the phone that a lady is dead under the big tree.

I'm in denial that the woman who gave me life is gone from the world. I'm not crying. I imagine I will cry later, at her funeral. It's hard to cry when none of it is real. If it were real, I would be crying. The damn shaking won't stop. The sweat won't stop dripping, and I look at my dad. I can't let Kelly use my father against me.

When I get my shit together and process everything, I will need to show the police everything I have. I couldn't save mom, but now I need to save all my energy to protect dad and save Jeremy.

My dad's shirt is covered in blood. He shakes from his forehead to his feet. His goosebumps are raised from the horrifying scene of my mother. The paramedics arrive at the same time as the cops.

I hold my mom's hand, and the warmness it had hours earlier is fleeting. Darkness is sinking in, and the paramedics encourage us to leave her body. That's when the tears come.

All the regrets I had in our relationship surface. The big tree is a place I can never come to again. But, when Jeremy gets out of college, the bigger tree at the community college can be our new perch. Our new world and haven.

All the photos my mother wanted to take won't happen. It's all my fault. I shouldn't have been so hard on her about my social media accounts. Did she know I loved her and all of her quirks in all of our fighting? Did mommy know anything? I was too busy trying to save Jeremy. I didn't think Kelly would kill my mom.

I should have been more resourceful. I should have been more strategic. Instead, she killed Gerald McLaren and put Jeremy Davis behind bars. And now my mother is dead at her hands, and she still got away.

I didn't even try to follow after her. I didn't try to strangle her and tackle her to the ground. The shock was too great that I froze like a pathetic statue. Being a statue is a useless thing when a crisis is at hand.

The paramedics take my mother's body away. I'm convinced she's dead. All her blood remains on the grass. The last warmth of my mother's body waters the earth with its *Scarlett death*.

My dad has a paramedic attempting to do deep breathing exercises with him. The cops want to ask us questions, but my dad refuses. How can one answer questions when it all happened so fast? It happened faster than I ever thought possible. Kelly was in a tree-like leopard, ready to pounce on its prey. I let it happen. I let it all happen.

Gerald McLaren is dead because of me. He wanted to apologize to me, and Jeremy will take the truth to his grave. My mother is dead because I am her daughter, Lily Green. Kelly has made it her sole duty to eliminate the people I care about the most.

Officer Reynolds is among the cops the show up in Harris Park. His tiny deputy stands beside him with his newly grown mustache. I don't want to be interviewed about my mother. So, all I will tell them is the truth that Kelly needs to be taken down.

"Lily Green, I have a few questions for you."

"No...my mother was just murdered. I am not talking to you right now. If you want to know who it was...go find Kelly Butterfield."

Officer Reynolds nods and understands that I need my space.

"Thanks for the lead. We will talk later after you've had time to make a statement. We have reason to believe that Kelly Butterfield was involved in the murder of Gerald McLaren. If you see Kelly anytime soon, please call us immediately. She is a wanted woman. I also want to let you know I have news about your boyfriend, Jeremy Davis."

The tears I shed for my mother make Officer Reynolds look blurry and hazy. I lean in to show Officer Reynolds that I need good news about my boyfriend. He has no good news for me. Nobody does, not really, not ever.

"What," I ask, impatiently wanting to cry for mom but holding back for Jeremy?

"Jeremy Davis is in the hospital. He tried to commit suicide last night in his jail cell."

Death takes on many forms. It takes our mothers away before our eyes. It poisons the thoughts of our boyfriends. Death always wins, but we have the power to decide if he will succeed in some cases. My mother didn't win against Death. He cheated and let another person murder my mother on his behalf. But for Jeremy, it isn't too late, I may have lost my mom, but I can't lose Jeremy Davis too. If I lose them all, I'll never be myself again.

Sparrows

Silence is the golden standard that surrounds our house. Dads decided to hold off on having a funeral. He doesn't know how to move on and how to process everything. I've removed pictures of mom around the house, so dad gets a break from seeing her face. I've transferred schools to an online high school finishing program.

With mom dead and only one parent remaining, I've decided to watch dad like a hawk night and day. But, at least with dad alive and well, I will be able to move forward. Someday, my dad will do the famous daddy-daughter dance with me when I get married. It's sad to think that mom will never be there for the occasion.

Mom will never talk to me again. She's never going to give me advice or take embarrassing photos of me ever again.

Mr. Davis and my dad have become good friends. They've come to understand the absence of family members and have found a friendship through grief. Dad grieves mom, and Mr. Davis misses his son.

The world doesn't like to be kind to my family. But, if I close my eyes, I am more appreciative of the times I had with my mother. I remember in the fourth grade. I had a high fever of 102 degrees. My mom picked me up, and instead of going home, she pushed me in a stroller around the zoo. She told me that fresh air was good for me, but she just wanted more time with me. I would give anything to have a fever and go to the zoo with her one more time.

The zoo reminds me of Jeremy. That was his community service duty for supposedly burning the church down. That should be Kelly's work. She's the one who should have shoveled camel shit for the summer, not Jeremy. And now he's in the slammer like a criminal.

Bitterness tastes like sour apples, the green ones that look good at first but taste like *Sour Patch Kids*. I find envelopes full of photos, some I recognize and others I don't. The one's I don't are moments in my childhood that my mother and father would know more about than me.

An unfinished scrapbook lies in the back of mom's old closet. It has a large pink bow and says, "*Congratulations, Lily*" on the top. Mom was making a surprise scrapbook for me. I had no idea. The school bus photo is toward the back of the scrapbook with a message from Mrs. Norris, the school bus driver. It says:

Dear Lily,

Congrats on graduating. I loved driving you to school. I will miss you telling me about your favorite romance novels.

Love,
Mrs. Norris

Even in her death, my mom surprises me. She took an embarrassing situation with the photo and attempted to make it better and less uncomfortable. I suspect this scrapbook would have been her peace offering to me if she had been allowed to live. Instead, I take scissors and glue and cut more pictures out. I spend the rest of the afternoon crying, weeping, and going down memory lane. Memory lane is where my mother lives; she lives in my thoughts, speaks in the videos we have left, and appears in our saved photos. Her spirit hasn't been killed. Only her physical self is gone. That in itself is comforting.

A sparrow lands on the tree outside the window as the first few snowflakes of the year appear. The snow comes late here, it's almost Christmas break, and the world has fallen apart. I have gained a boyfriend, dealt with a bully, and lost a mother in a single semester. I will miss fighting with my mom. I will miss her taking care of me when I get sick.

Sparrows were mom's favorite bird. They represented going home for her. Sparrows build nests in the beautiful places of the world I have never seen. I like to think this sparrow is my mother's spirit coming to me and telling me it will be okay. I believe in signs and believe they exist in nature to keep us going in this mess we call a world.

"Hello, mom," I say as a tear falls on my face. More fall like the heavy rains of the deep Amazon jungle. Rain is gentle and then falls all at once. When it comes all at once, I collapse with it.

The sparrow chirps back, and I know that it's my mother calling to me from her new home, in her heaven up above. My mom is a sparrow, and she can finally fly free without a care in the world. She raised me well and asked for forgiveness in death. I only wish she were alive, so I could tell her I forgive her and am sorry.

Prepare to Die

Ringing in my ears like the hum of a thousand bees pollinating in summer. Ringing from my teeth clenching as tight as they will go. The grinding of my teeth has worn down my back wisdom teeth. Without my braces in the way and a fresh new clean smile...All I do is clench. I think about everything from the Lending Library carrying many stories to the books I donated to its collection. The very collection I once donated *The History of Pirates* too.

I would travel the sea and let my bullies walk the plank if I were Anne Bonnie. But instead, I clench my jaw at the very thing creating my panic and terror.

Kelly's picture stares at me through the pages of my old yearbook. Her middle school photo had braces, but hers were invisible. People didn't dare call her names even then. If any girl said anything about that, she'd give you a horsey with your bra strap so powerful that your back would have whip marks until freshman year.

Anne Bonnie would have pulled the trigger and would still get to celebrate her mother on Mother's Day. My mother's blood is still present under my fingernails. I haven't been able to wash it out. All I do is scrub and rinse no matter how hard I try. The smell of my mother's last DNA lives beneath my nails. As if I'm the one who murdered her in her wake. Like Lady Macbeth, all I can do is sit and wonder. Lady Macbeth murdered King Duncan in that play. I remember Mr. Cronkwright talking about it endlessly in Freshmen Brit Lit three years ago.

Lady Macbeth was guilty of murder and went insane and imagined blood on her hands. My mother's blood is real, but like Lady Macbeth, I, too, want the blood out.

The notes from Kelly's and Jeremy's letters call to me. As I sit on my bed staring at Kelly's middle school braces photo, I remember why I don't like her to begin with. The mockery and the teasing are all very hard for me to wrap my head around. She wrote crude messages and drew mean plots on the bathroom stalls. She would write with lipstick on mirrors and never got caught. I knew it was her in eighth grade, but she never got ratted out. No one catches Kelly in a criminal act.

The private messages of her threat to my parents burn my fingers with a fiery revenge. I open the box under the bed and pull all the evidence out—the drawings of her plots on me, the Vineyard church plot, and Jeremy's letter of testimony. It's all going to the police station. It's about time someone set the record straight.

I should have presented this to the police earlier. But I thought I could outsmart Kelly, and that was my mistake. My mother is dead because I thought I could trap a lion in a sheep's pen. The lion won, and I am still cleaning up the remaining blood in my claws.

The pictures of mom I took down from the walls are stacked in piles around my room. The presence of mom is everywhere as I hear a sparrow chirp by the window. It's late, and hearing a sparrow chirp at night means it's mom talking to me or all in my head.

The following day comes, and the sparrow sings its song of depression. It's my mother telling me she believes in Jeremy's alibi. He did not murder Gerald McLaren, and he didn't burn the church down.

"Dad, I'm going out for a while. Are you going to be okay," I ask, wondering if our house is safe or booby-trapped? Nothing feels safe anymore. Not even safety feels safe. Safety is a pretend state of being created by adults to force children to be calm 75% of the time in the waves of life. But, boy, was that sure clever of them to invent that great lie.

"Okay. See you soon. Can you order the flowers for your mom's funeral? I can't look at all this stuff. It's hard for me," dad says, unsure of what to say. How does a father react to his child who has lost a parent?

"Sure, dad, I will handle the funeral arrangements. I've decided to go to the community college and take general education classes since mom is gone and you'd be alone. I figured you'd need my company, you know?" I tell him with a singsong hum in my voice. I used to speak this way as a young child to let dad know I needed his approval.

"Sure, honey. Thanks for thinking of me. Do you think Jeremy will be in prison for a long time?"

"No."

"Why not," dad asks, with coffee in his hand and a picture of my mom in the other? The photo has coffee stains dripping from the sides.

"I'm going to the police station. I have evidence...that could help Jeremy get out. I showed mom the night before Kelly...hurt her. And she believes he is innocent."

I show dad everything. Keeping this to myself was why his wife was murdered under the big tree at Harris Park.

"You can't show this to them, Lily. So, what good will it do?"

"Mom believed me, and I know that it will all be okay again if I could just see Officer Reynolds."

My throat jumps up and down. Finally, I choke on my words, and dad doesn't deny me the truth.

"Going to the police with evidence won't bring mom back."

"You don't think I know that, dad? But it might bring Jeremy, my suicidal boyfriend home. And if I can save him from himself, then I will do that. So excuse me, dad. I have evidence the police need right away."

Dad steps aside and lets me out the door. He can't stop me when I am on a mission. Being on a mission means I have a place to go and a plan to achieve.

My mother's favorite movie was the *Princess Bride,* and like Inigo Montoya from that movie, he wanted to revenge his father's death. So, I, too, want Kelly to prepare to die.

I drive the car to the police station with all the evidence in the passengers' seat. I was so paranoid that I would destroy the evidence that I put it all in Ziplocs to ensure it wouldn't get wet.

While on my way to the station, I get a call from Mr. Davis. I pull the car over and open it.

"Hello, is everything okay, Mr. Davis," I ask?

I hear a loud breath and three short ones follow.

"Jeremy is in the hospital. He tried to hang himself last night."

All the Feels

The ghost with no face wears a hood. He passes through fog and dances on the other side of the clouds. When he comes to earth, he sleeps in caves. Caves cast their shadows against the crackling fires of hope. Hope is all that remains for Jeremy Davis. The sun is a fleeting idea that hides behind the clouds in their dark black sky.

I never knew what living in crisis mode was like. It sucks and hurts my skin. Everything hurts my soul, my heart, my spirit. Pain has many forms and many faces, and I can't bear to wear my masks any longer. I've become a castle with one bridge to the world on the other side. When Jeremy's father told me he tried to commit suicide, that bridge fell into the world of bullies.

Armor can protect a knight for so long. The helmet protects his thoughts. Jeremy's helmet was tossed aside ages ago. To me, he is like the *Green Knight*, tossing aside fear and worry.

The keys to my car fall to the floor. Damn! Getting to Jeremy is all I care about in this moment. Not seeing Jeremy for endless days is not what I thought it would be. It's been a great emptiness escaping into the hallways of everything else.

When a prisoner needs to go to the hospital, everyone guards them like an infant in time out. The envelope of evidence sits in the front seat of my car. Instead of heading to the police station, the hospital calls my name.

I never knew the ravens would sing my way as passionately as they do now. Ravens are the vocalists of death. They call her and invite her in. Only those who have seen death can see ravens and can be mocked by their presence.

The ravens in my head swarm around the hospital. The walk to the hospital is strenuous. I didn't get to go with mom to the hospital. She was dead long before they took her. She died in my lap as her blood dripped its last remaining warmth on my legs. This is a different type of death. It's the death of almost.

When 'almost' happens, it can become a shit show, and the world could end. My heart can't bear to have Jeremy die. If he does die like my mom, it will be the end of me. The back of my mind will spiral into a closed-minded existence.

The hospital grows out of the ground in a tall building with a thousand windows for a thousand patients. I only care about one, and he might be dead by the time I enter. The ravens flying above the hospital flock, and our eyes meet. They come toward me, getting ready to peck.

I know it's not real, but it's real enough that I duck. Officer Reynolds finds me and sees my frightened face.

"Lily, is that you? They told me you'd be coming to see him. It doesn't look good. He's barely awake. Your father told me you had something to give me."

I hand Officer Reynolds my car keys and tell him to grab the box of envelopes. The keys jingle as he opens the car door again.

"What is this?"

"Evidence. That proves Jeremy never did any of those horrible things everyone thought he did. My mom believed him, but Kelly murdered my mom, and now you have to take my word for it. From Kelly's plans to Jeremy's confession, it's all in there. So it's not like it will matter if Jeremy is dead. That's what they wanted, though, isn't it?"

"Lily, we can talk about this later. And I'm sorry about your mother. We've been trying to find Kelly since your mother died. We haven't been able to. So, the important thing for you to do right now is find Jeremy."

I know he's right. All I want to do is see Jeremy.

My heart throbs in my ribs. Its ripple effect makes me nervous. I haven't been this anxious to see someone in a long time. I haven't seen Jeremy in weeks. He doesn't know my mom is dead, and I don't even know if he's alive. The walking of my feet is heavy. Each step is like heavy snowshoes that grip the hospital floor with grief.

Being everything all at once is the hardest thing I've ever done. Becoming a bottle and capping the lid is a bad idea, but it's all I can do to keep myself from crying. When all the feels come and find me in the darkest of closets. She's like the sparrow at my window. When the big tree at Harris Park sways in the autumn breeze, that's her voice drifting in the wind-whispering that she is proud of me.

The steps toward the hospital hallway last forever. The clicking of shoes, and crying of babies, and the chewing of gum make my teeth clench deeper and tighter.

The elevator door dings, and the doors open. I scuff my feet inside and press the button for the 4th floor. The fourth floor is where all the feels live. Where worry meets romance and sorrow meets joy. I'm angry at Jeremy and saddened by him as well.

The place where all the feels lie,

All these feels make me cry,

The spaces inside my mind,

I can't go back and rewind,

Over time, I hope you heal,

As I mourn with all the feels...

The door to Jeremy's hospital room is bitter from the phantoms of failure. He's let me down because he wanted to be gone. He wanted to clock out before our lips could meet and our lives could start. He wanted to be six feet under away from me.

The vital signs go up and down, and his eyes are barely open. The tiger marks from his blades are still seen through the tubes and breathing machine wires. No one knows where they all go or what body part they are saving. It doesn't matter, though, because no matter how they help him, at his core, Jeremy Davis may never let me in.

The cops guard the hospital door and let me in.

"Hi, Lily."

How can he say 'hi' to me like he's been available to go on dates with? Like we are two people with no pain between us.

"Don't *hi*, me. You scared me. Did you know my mother died? Kelly stabbed her by the tree in Harris Park. And you try to end it all, and all you can say is 'hi, Lily?' That's not fair. You don't get to do that to me."

His smile disappears. Maybe I've said too much, but it's not fair. I'm in love with a boy who hates himself.

"I'm sorry, Lily. I wasn't trying to scare you. Everything felt hopeless, like no one would believe me. I didn't do any of it..."

"My mom died believing you. She read the letter you wrote me. I gave all of it away."

Jeremy coughs and grabs his neck. The redness of his neck shows me how he tried to end his life. He tried to cut his breathing off with suffocation. His breath could have ended, and his life could have been gone. But, instead, his heart is still beating, forcing him to be here with me.

When the days of our lives seem too hard to go on,

When we take our fate into our hands because these days feel too long,

Remember to feel every tear that comes to your face,

Remember to stare up at planets dancing up in space,

When you look up and feel the last breath of the spring,

That's where you and I will be together through everything,

Everything brings out the shades of red, white, and blue,

Everything blossoms with the hues of loving you,

When my happiness is the closeness of us,

Remember that one day we will return to dust,

Being together is our forever, so go and pick up your heels,

So, we can fall in love again with all our passion and all the feels...

The tears on my face are saltier than oceans. Bigger than droplets crying for Jeremy. The red of my eyes match the red marks on his neck, where the rope almost had him. I walk toward the hospital bed and sit by his side. My tears are wiped away by Jeremy's hand.

His touch triggers the best parts of us. The us we could return to, if only he agreed to get help.

"I'm sorry about your mom. And thanks for telling me she believes me."

"I showed my dad your confession letter and gave everything to Officer Reynolds."

I tell him about my mother dying in her puddle of blood. The horrible messages Kelly sent me and the threats on their lives. I stay with Jeremy all day. The cops talk amongst themselves outside and point at us.

What they think doesn't matter. I have my Jeremy, and I kiss Jeremy with salty tears on my lips. My kiss shocks him, but he returns the kiss with tears in his eyes. Somewhere within his soul, Jeremy knows that I love and forgive him. I only hope that that's enough for him to keep going a little longer so we can live with our pain, joy, and sadness and live together with all the feels.

Of Life and Death

Graveyards are the final resting place for the dead. They are where the endless souls dance for eternity under a moonlit forever. The souls of the cemetery held onto Jeremy but didn't take him down into the land of Hades. He fought, and he held onto life just for me. Death is where the ravens swirl in their endless circles. Hunger finds them, and nails dig into their prey. We are all called by death in the end. The grim reaper himself holds his scythe and carries it along as a walking stick. Walking sticks are used to guide souls on the path to Hades. If I discover Hades, I will find my mom. I will find her there beneath the bones of her final breath.

All the feels take away my breath,
When funerals approach and force me to face death,
I think of the heavens parting like glass,
Hoping her last days have come at last,
The grim reaper is a soul deliverer taking souls away,
If he walks too far into the depths, the souls will try to stay,
There lies a place between the living and the dead,
That's where I want to meet her as I sleep in bed,
In the land of half-asleep, I am half-awake,
With my eyes half crying, I feel my heartbreak,
The land of half-asleep is where I say, "Goodbye, Mom,"
I wake with my eyes both red. It's time to move on,
The place where all the feels spin inside my head,
And only on angel wings can I rise from my bed.

My whole life, people have told me how brave I am. But I don't believe them. Being brave means one has courage. I'm not courageous enough to graduate without my mother there. Sure, we had our fights. Our ups and downs got the better of us. But, life has a way of standing still and moving the earth out of orbit. When the ground stops spinning, and the world knows it, that's when I will see her soul before the funeral. I want to honor my mother and remember her well. But I can't get closure if I don't face death. The only way to face death is to talk about it in the most honest of ways.

The person I love the most wanted to end his life. He wanted to end his before he knew my mother was gone. If he had known that my mother was gone, would he have fought more and waited for me? His attempt at dying failed, but his desire to be gone was the strongest I have ever witnessed it to be.

Will talking to Jeremy about his desire to die help me understand my mom's parting? Maybe not. My mother is up there somewhere dancing with the eagles. She stretches her wings and takes flight with the sparrows. The angels are teaching her how to use her wings, so she can guide the souls to where they need to be. I don't know what is true about death. My family didn't raise me to believe in God or anything. We went to the Vineyard church on occasion with my grandparents. But my parents never prepared me for death.

The only other death I remember is Uncle Daniel's. We didn't go to the funeral. We just left a card with our sympathies on the front porch of Aunt Mille's house. I wasn't close to Uncle Daniel, so I didn't feel anything for his death. But for my mother, I bear confusion and wear it like a robe. My grief runs deep within my veins, and the only way to understand death is to interview him.

Jeremy, my sweet love, I wish you never tried to kill yourself. It's made my faith shake and my trust in us crumble. I don't believe he ever wanted to fall in love with me in the first place. We didn't plan for it to happen. It just did. He was in love once before, but we are deeper than that. The only problem is our roots of love weren't deep enough to stop him from almost committing suicide.

Death confuses everything within me. One minute a person you care about is here, and the next, their physical body is no more. I'd like to believe my grandma when she tells me that everyone has a soul that goes to heaven. But instead, I want to think that my mother is in the sky dancing with the sparrows beside pearly white gates.

I sit up in my bed. After visiting Jeremy in the hospital yesterday, I came home and cried. I cried because of mom. I threw up because of Jeremy. Between murder and an almost death, I've completely lost my appetite.

At some point in the night, dad must have tucked me in. I know Kelly is still out there. But I am too tired to face her now. I want to think she is the reason that Jeremy almost died. It would be easy to blame her when she's the reason my mom is no more. Jeremy got in trouble with the law because part of her influence may have triggered him. But his flirtation with death has existed for a while now. He told me about his mom and her abusive boyfriends that wouldn't leave him alone.

My parents never got divorced. I will never know what it feels like to see parents fall out of love with each other. However, given that my mother is dead, I think I'd prefer they have divorced because at least I would still be witnessing her breathing.

I rise from bed and collect myself. I get ready as best as I can and return to the hospital. My mother's funeral is in a few days. I can't face her death without understanding Jeremy's. The electric doors to the hospital part like the seas of Egypt.

Officer Reynolds has accommodated my visits with Jeremy over the last few days. I've even invited him to the funeral to keep an eye on Jeremy. Since Jeremy is still being investigated, who knows if the evidence I gave them is good enough. Maybe it is, and they are waiting to tell me until after the funeral. However, the police have agreed to keep an eye on Jeremy so he can attend the funeral. It's not ideal, but it sure beats him staying in prison and missing everything.

I'm hoping the funeral doesn't trigger Jeremy's relationship with death. I don't understand how he and death came to be friends. In some corner of the world, death sits and waits for Jeremy to call. I hope Jeremy ignores his phone that day, so Jeremy and I can be together a bit longer.

I get to Jeremy's hospital room. He still looks like the Frankenstein monster plugged into every machine, like a human cell phone. The marks on his neck are covered in bandages today. He looks better than I thought he would. He is sitting up in the hospital bed, eating pudding.

"Good morning, Lily. Officer Reynolds just told me you want me to go to your mother's funeral. I'm sorry about her death, by the way. I can't remember if I said that or not already."

I sit beside Jeremy and touch his hands. His normal warmth that's familiar has returned. My eyes feel wet. I wasn't planning on starting our time together in tears. Instead, I cry in his arms.

"I'm sorry...I'm sad about my mom, you know? That's another reason why I came over today. I wanted to talk to you about death. I don't think I'll ever understand my mom's death hell; I don't even understand death. I've never been around it before. Sorry if I'm insensitive, Jeremy. I want to know, to understand it. I don't think I ever will."

"You came over to talk about death? I'm not sure I'm the person who should be telling you about this...given...what I almost...did."

Jeremy chokes on those last few words. It only makes me snuggle into his chest more.

"I love you, Jeremy." That is the only response I have to offer him—the corners of his mouth smile. I haven't seen his smile in a long time.

"I don't deserve you after what I almost did. Thanks for sticking beside me. I want you to know. Officer Reynolds has been really helpful to my dad and me. He's working on the evidence you gave them. I think it might help. I'm enrolling in a program for people who are suicidal. It's basically counseling. It's a start, Lily. I'm trying to get on my feet again. In that split second before my life almost ended, I realized that I didn't want to die. I want to live to see you again. You brought me out of my shell and made me come alive again. If you want to understand death, live your life and mean something to people, Lily. Grow old and make memories, so people will celebrate how much they love you when it's time for your funeral. I think that's how you understand death. You keep breathing and keep pushing forward every day until your last breath. While I was experiencing my almost final moments, I saw angels. They rescued me, Lily. They raised me and brought me back. Perhaps, I was dead for a minute. I will never know. But I'm here now. There are wonderful things on the other side of life, but those angels reminded me that there's a reason to keep on living. My reason is you, Lily Green."

In a single breath, Jeremy has told me the truth about death. He's shown me his experience, so I can move past the hurt and celebrate my mom. Her time ended before it should have. But he's right. I need to keep pushing forward. That's what mom would have wanted.

"My reason is you, Jeremy Davis." I look at Jeremy with all the tubes and wires going everywhere, and they make him beautiful. He almost died, but now he is free of it. I'm glad he's getting help. I squeeze his hand, and he interlocks our fingers. His lips find mine and startle me. The warmth of his lips tells me he is alive and to keep pushing forward. I kiss him back, grateful for our time on earth together.

Jitters

"It's nice to kiss you without your braces on. I always knew you were pretty, but now all you are is beautiful," Jeremy says as we split up from our kiss.

I say goodbye to him and head out of the hospital. Hospitals represent life and death. They are places where people try their best to cling to life. But life is a sacred thing, and the doctor, along with the angels, kept my Jeremy safe so he could help me out today.

The drive home is terrifying. All I can think about is Kelly. I am at peace with everything else but her. I want her to be put in her place. She hides in the shadows and waits like an eel ready to strike. I haven't been to school in weeks. I can't stomach the KAT trio. All three girls have been arrested and are suspects in the murder trial of Gerald McLaren. It puts my mind at ease that they are being held accountable for something they have done.

But I still can't go back to that school and finish what I've started. I can't return to tutoring. I can't walk past the big tree in Harris Park without thinking of my mother's death or getting egged by bullies. But, most of all, I can't do it without Jeremy. Mr. Davis won't let Jeremy return to school, especially now that he has a criminal record and is a suspect in a murder case.

With the arrest of the KAT trio, the police have decided to allow Jeremy to return home. However, he is now under house arrest and wears an ankle monitor that tells them that he hasn't left the property. To Jeremy, it's the freedom to be home and out of the hospital. To me, it's an improvement, and I hope that he will be free in the not-too-distant future.

The only exception for Jeremy to leave the house is to attend my mother's funeral, with Officer Reynolds as his escort. And if there's a house fire.

Other than that, Jeremy is stuck at home. His dad lets him watch tv and play video games as much as he wants. His dad is just happy he is out of the slammer.

Jeremy will be finishing up school online. Like me, he, too, won't be returning to the physical hallways of Ashmore Highschool. I am eager to get this school year done and over with. I often go to Jeremy's house to tutor him and help him study for his ACTs.

My dad has postponed my mother's funeral by a few months. He's not ready to talk about how she died. Instead, he wants to talk about how she lived and loved everyone she met through her love of photography. Her love of the camera was always invasive but is greatly missed by me. I have started to document my own life in my newly found blog in her absence.

I've started a suicide prevention and awareness blog. In it, I interview survivors and tell their stories. I've also made interview videos that I've been attaching to my blog. It's gotten some attention from a few colleges that want me to be the club president of the suicide squad of Ashmore College. I haven't accepted the role because, to me, that role should be filled by Jeremy. Of the two of us, he's taken this chance of sitting at home to do something meaningful with his life. He's been writing an autobiography called *The Life I Almost Ended*. It's his confession and testimony to his spiraling and daily battles with mental health. I can't wait to read it.

Ashmore College has asked him to speak to the incoming first-year students about his struggles. He's considered it. Assuming he is allowed to live his life, they find the KAT trio guilty of all crimes committed. Life isn't perfect, but healing comes with many faces. Sometimes you're up, and sometimes you are stuck in the big messy middle. The big middle is the valley between the mountains. Although it's not the best or worst of places, it is a neutral place.

Finding Kelly wasn't easy. The cops had to start at the big tree in Harris Park. They found her hiding in the ruins of the burned-down Vineyard church. They said finding her there wasn't a coincidence. It put her at the scene of the crime. It made her even more guilty than Jeremy. It meant she knew something and that she was involved. The officer to arrest her was Officer Reynolds.

Three weeks pass. It's April. The end of the school year is around the corner. My online classes are endless. Government is fun to take. Learning about congress makes me want to revisit Washington DC. I haven't been since mom took me and made me tour the Holocaust Museum. The museum was eye-opening and made me feel guilty I ate food that morning.

I sprawl out on Jeremy's couch. I still live with my dad. Since mom died, and it felt like my fault for her death, I moved back home to be with dad. I didn't want him to be alone and be victimized by Kelly.

"Lily, are you going to go home soon? You've been studying for your ACTs all evening."

"I'm taking the SAT. And I don't even care how I do on them. I'm sure I will do good enough. I've already been accepted into the community college. I'm taking the SAT just in case I want to transfer later. I'm just not ready to be far away from my dad yet."

"That makes sense. I don't blame you for that. I'm so sorry about the loss of your mom. I'm sure they will find Kelly guilty, given you and your dad witnessed her murder. Surely, they can't ignore eyewitness accounts. Are you going to have to testify in the trial against Kelly," Jeremy asks?

With everything else going on, I haven't considered the possibility of testifying against Kelly and in front of her. It's a terrifying thought. But one that needs time and preparation if I am to honor my mother correctly.

It's not just about facing Kelly and feeling brave. It's about knowing I can look her in the eye and tell her why she is wrong. This trial is for my mother's death, Gerald McLaren, and setting the universe right for Jeremy. I might never eat eggs again, but it might feel nice to look at Kelly in the face and show the world that she did it and that bullying is wrong.

This is a trial for the victims. The people who have been blamed for doing nothing wrong. All the wrongdoings in this town start and end with the

KAT trio. I don't care what happens with Amy and Tia. But Kelly is the queen of the chessboard, and putting her in checkmate with the help of the justice system will be very rewarding.

My mother won't be here to see me challenge my bully. This trial is a reason to call her out in the brightest of rooms and tell the jury the truth. My mother was murdered in cold blood, I miss my mom, and I only hope to make her proud of me when I share my witness of bullying, murder, and injustice. Her reign of terror will end in that courtroom. I only hope that my head will be held up high when it does.

The Trial

Time has slowed down. All my dreams are in red. Red is the color of roses and the color of blood. Both describe my mother. Blood for her death and roses for her grave. Blood at her murder scene and roses at her funeral.

When I dream in red, I don't sleep well. The dreams always end with Kelly laughing. Last night, I didn't dream about my mother. Instead, I dreamed about Gerald McLaren. He was standing in the ruins of the Vineyard church, holding eggs. He threw the eggs to the side and hugged me. He apologized to me for bullying me. I forgave him, and then Kelly entered my dream. I woke up panicked. Being covered in sweat in my bed is a horrible sticky feeling.

"Lily, are you okay? I heard screaming," dad says, rushing into my room.

His coffee spills a little on the side and moves around in his mug. Since mom died, dad has been sporting an ugly red bathrobe that retired in the 1960s. Pretty sure my dad inherited it from his old man. It hasn't been washed since the Pharaohs ruled Egypt.

"Yes, I just had a nightmare. Nothing to worry about."

"Sweetie, you've been having a lot of nightmares since mom died. Do you need to talk to someone? I can get you counseling, or maybe the school has someone you can talk to," Dad asks while scratching his head?

I'm used to dad scratching his head like ideas will come rushing at him, scratching the side. He's convinced his brain is like a genie lamp. The more he scratches, the more possible light bulb moments will appear.

"No, it's okay, dad. I'll be fine. I just need to get this trial over with. I don't want to face Kelly. I don't think I'm strong enough to do this."

Dad sits beside me on the bed and puts his hand on my shoulder like he used to when I was a little girl.

"You don't have to do this alone, sweetheart. You have me here with you. I can testify about your mother's murder. All I want you to focus on is telling the Judge what happened to you the day you got egged by the tree."

I look down. I don't want to think about being egged. That was a miserable day. I should have kept that day to myself. I wish mom never found me like that at all. If she never saw me, perhaps she'd be alive now. Being bullied for another semester would have been worth the price of my mother being alive some more.

"I don't want to go at all." The trial is this afternoon. The more I think about going. The colder my feet become. Cold feet happen to people who are scared and want to get out of things. And it's tied shoes I will be sporting all afternoon.

I put my hands over my face and take a deep breath. My chest rises slowly as the air expands within my lungs. I release the air in a controlled fashion while counting down from ten in my head. I do this five times, and the tears still come. The burning sensation of tears returns to my eyes. All I know is how to cry. Tears fall like flowing water descending a mountain.

Dad's hand reassures me that he, too, misses mom. His hand on my shoulder becomes a hug. A hug becomes a sniffle. And a sniffle becomes a cry. We get lost in our rainstorm. Finally, the clouds part, and we collect ourselves.

The morning drags on, and we get ready for the afternoon trial. I've never been to a courtroom. But I've seen enough on tv to build up an image in my head. It all smells like wood and antique shops. The building is old and covered in ivy and bricks.

No phones. No technology. No devices are allowed inside. I feel like I'm entering one of the settings of my books from the Lending Library. I hope to include this courtroom in my story if I ever write novels. It might help me process all I am going through.

Hundreds of Ashmore students and parents fill the courtroom. The benches and pews all fill up quickly. Students in the audience are wearing t-shirts supporting Gerald McLaren. Others think Kelly did it, and some believe Jeremy is at fault.

Members of the Vineyard Church are in the audience. Even Mr. Cronkwright made it. The hardest part for me is seeing Jeremy wearing handcuffs like he did something wrong. The only thing that makes me feel better is knowing Officer Reynolds sits beside Jeremy. I think deep down. He will prove Jeremy's innocence. And perhaps he will fight for that.

The KAT trio sits on the opposite side of the courtroom. I feel Kelly's gaze at the side of my face. If our eyes meet, I will never be able to testify against Kelly. Everything about Kelly scares me. Her eyes, her voice, and her breath. The dragon in the room with no empathy to be found anywhere.

Lawyers speak legalese. The Judge coughs. And I still have no idea what's going on. The jury looks bored. I can't help but think they have decided Jeremy's fate before listening to this trial.

Kelly is brought to the stand. She swears on the Bible that she will tell the truth. That girl will never tell the truth, even under oath. The crowd leans in like it's a play or drama to watch. It's all disgusting to me. My mother's death is a spectacle to keep them entertained. Jeremy's suicidal ways worry me today. The verdict might determine if he will stay just for me. He said I am his reason to go on, but is it enough?

"Kelly Butterfield, you are accused of murder for Layla Green and Gerald McLaren. You are also accused of burning down the Vineyard church, destroying school property, and bullying Lily Green. How do you plea?"

"Not guilty," Kelly says.

They bring out the evidence I gave to Officer Reynolds.

"Are you aware of the contents of this evidence? Have you seen these items before," The Judge asks?

"I've never seen any of that before." Kelly lies through her teeth.

"Your DNA was found on the murder weapon for Layla Green. Layla Green was stabbed to death by this knife. We also found your DNA on the gun used to kill Gerald McLaren. Members of the jury, we will now hear one key witness to the murder of Layla Green. I call Jared Green to the stand."

They remove Kelly from the stand. My dad gets up and swears on the Bible. My dad is not a very religious man. He grew up going to church. But his faith never stuck. His faith burned down with the Vineyard church of his youth.

"Jared Green, tell us how your wife died."

"Yes, your honor. My wife...well, she was stabbed in broad daylight by Kelly. We were attending a yoga class that Saturday. Then out of nowhere, Kelly comes. She stabbed my wife in front of the tree on the picnic blanket beneath the branches."

They show the jury the pictures of my mother's body beneath the tree on a big projector—the memories of that day flood back. Jeremy's jaw drops as he sees the horrifying images. I look down. I don't want to relive that day. They remove the pictures as the jury takes their notes.

My dad leaves the stand. The Judge calls Jeremy to the stand.

"Jeremy Davis, you have been accused of murdering Gerald McLaren and burning down the Vineyard church. However, after thoroughly examining the evidence, your DNA was not found on the murder weapon. How do you plea?"

"I don't know how to answer that question. I didn't murder Gerald McLaren. But the Vineyard Church did burn to the ground. And I was there inside. That day is all a blur to me, your honor."

Officer Reynolds walks up to the Judge and gives him the note Jeremy wrote to me as his confession.

"According to this note written in your hand, it states that Kelly and her gang framed you. Is that accurate?"

"Yes, it is your honor. I wanted to kill myself that day. I wanted to break my neck from the church rafters, but they interrupted my attempt. The only reason I'd ever want to hurt any of them is that they made my girlfriend, Lily Green, feel so awful about herself. Lily wanted to protect me from myself. But then, I saw Kelly shoot Gerald McLaren."

The Judge and Jeremy speak for another ten minutes. Jeremy's testimony impresses the jury, who continues to take their notes. Finally, the Judge calls for a recess. I am tired from all the focusing and concentrating I have had to do today. It feels like multiple trials at once. With them being so interconnected, we had to get them out of the way today. This could take several days, for all I know.

During the break, Officer Reynolds finds me.

"You don't have to come to the stand. You don't have to if you don't want to. We have enough evidence to lock Kelly up."

If I don't tell her how I feel now, she will go to prison, knowing I was a coward.

"No, I want to say something to her. Just this once."

Officer Reynolds understands and finds the Judge. The recess is over, and I am called to the stand.

"Lily Green, you are being called to the stand because you have requested to say a few words to Kelly."

"Yes, your honor. Kelly, my whole life, you have tormented me and bullied me. You took my mom from me. And I will never forgive you for that. But I want you to know that you have not won. When I look at the sky, my mother looks at me, and she is free. When Jeremy smiles at me, he is free. When you get locked up, I am sure you will think of me every day. But after today, I will never think of you again."

It wasn't the speech I wrote. I wrote a five-page speech. I put a lot of thought into it. But ended up going off-script. However, the jury and Jeremy are happy with my words. Even dad has a half-smile showing.

Kelly is called back to the stand. The Judge prepares to give the verdict.

"Kelly, you have been found guilty on all accounts. You have been found guilty of the murder of Gerald McLaren. You have been found guilty of the murder of Layla Green. You have been found guilty of burning the Vineyard Church, destroying Ashmore Highschool property, and for bullying Lily Green. You will spend the next rest of your days behind bars."

Officer Reynolds takes Kelly away, who shouts, screams, and snorts my way.

"As for you, Jeremy Davis, you have been found innocent on all accounts. Therefore, the charges against you have been dropped, and you are free to go."

Jeremy smiles at me. Deep down, we know we have won. A mighty victory has been achieved by us underdogs in love. The officer removes the handcuffs and anklet from Jeremy's body. I run to him and kiss him for everyone to see in the courtroom. I don't care who sees. I don't care who knows that I, Lily Green am in love with Jeremy Davis. And being in love with someone like him makes me grateful to be alive.

The Ashmore Tree

Now that the trial is over, my life is a dream. Dreams exist above reality, just a little below perfection. The only person missing is mom. I will never hear her voice again. I will never listen to her say she loves me except in old voice mails and old videos.

The funeral is in a few days. I haven't cared about the funeral. I haven't wanted to plan anything. Planning the funeral means she really is gone. The way she died is so horrendous. I wish she fell asleep one night and didn't wake up. That would have been more tolerable.

With the trial being over, I have to face the parting clouds. When the clouds part, the truth is revealed. Sometimes truth is beautiful and sets us free. That's what the heavens did for Jeremy. They set him free above the angels. But for my mom, she dances with the sparrows, and I am here on earth to witness it.

Destiny lives with Father time. He can either change your fate, or he can let the cruelness of night rule with its blackness. The blessing he gave to me was Jeremy Davis. I now have more time, more time to get to know him. More time to love him with my entire being. More time to prepare for college.

The big tree in Harris Park is not for us. However, Jeremy promised me he'd show me the large new tree we'd enjoy together. The new tree for us is on the campus of Ashmore Community College. Ashmore is known for its trees. There are various maple trees all over campus. The leaves in fall are endless shades of red and orange like cathedrals extending upward beside the large education buildings.

I never thought I could be excited about college. I might study writing and become a novelist. Or maybe I will be a librarian. But instead, I am thinking of minoring in photography. It would help me get close to my mom. She's the reason for everything. Photography was her passion. If I studied, it would make missing her go away a little for me.

I pull the car up to Jeremy's house. His porch smells the way I have missed it, like Jeremy. It's nice to see him come out. His scars from his cutting days pop through his t-shirt. They will always be there but have been fading a little bit more. The rope scarred his neck. The rope burn reminds me that he almost didn't make it.

"Hey, Lily, are you ready to go to the big tree at Ashmore College?" Jeremy asks as he opens the passenger door. Although I wish Jeremy were driving, I want to focus on holding his hand and feeling its warmth beneath mine.

"Can you drive us there? I don't know the way." It's not entirely true. I have an idea where it is. But for now, I need to accept that Jeremy is breathing and is still with me.

"Sure, get out and give me the keys." I hand Jeremy the keys. He shows his whole face to me. The black hair he has isn't covering his eyes today.

"Can we get tattoos together?" I ask. I'm eighteen and think Jeremy needs a tattoo date with me.

"What do you want to get? I'm always down for a tattoo."

Do I really want to get a tattoo? What should I get?

"A sparrow. It would be in all black ink. I would get it on my right forearm." I point to my forearm and show Jeremy exactly how big I want my tattoo to be.

"I think I would get a semi-colon. On my left wrist," Jeremy says.

The semi-colon is a tattoo that has a significant meaning for suicide survivors. It means their life is like a sentence. It didn't end with a period. A semi-colon is a pause to take a breath in the sentence. That next breath means they are still here, pushing through, hoping to continue the next day and the day after that.

"I think that's a great tattoo to get, Jeremy. Let's get them today before we go to Ashmore College. I'm a little nervous to see the big tree if I am honest. Since my mother was murdered beneath one, I know it's not the same tree, but the memory is still there."

I click my heels against the grass. We haven't gotten in the car yet. I give Jeremy the car keys. He opens the door for me, and I get in. Off to the tattoo parlor, we go.

"I know the funeral will be hard for you. But I think closure is important. You faced Kelly. I saw you do that in a courtroom. I think you need to see the big tree at Ashmore College, so you will see for yourself that it's not the same tree. And why do you want to get a tattoo of a sparrow?"

"Sparrows were my mom's favorite birds. And lately, one has been watching over me at my parent's house. I think it's a sign that I'm supposed to get one and that my mom is watching out for me beyond the grave."

Jeremy holds my hand as we drive through the light green spring trees. April is almost perfect. The air is crisp but not too sweaty.

We get to *Marvelous Tattoo*. They accept walk-ins. We fill out forms that prove we are old enough to scar our bodies. They scan our licenses. A lady with both arms filled with tattoos greets us. She's wearing goth attire and has piercings in every location imaginable.

"Hi, I'm Abby. Who's going first?" I look at Jeremy. He sits down in the chair and shows Abby the semi-colon he wants to get. She finishes it in about thirty minutes. The tattoo machine sounds like a buzzing dentist's office. It sounds like all the dental drills are having a convention. The buzzing makes the goosebumps rise to the surface of my skin. I won't let cold feet stop me from getting the sparrow on my forearm.

Jeremy gets up and pats my butt. It's the first time he has ever done anything like that in public. I'm so embarrassed I hardly noticed the tattooist has started tattooing the sparrow on me. My sparrow takes an hour or so to complete.

Our tattoos are covered in plastic wrap to protect them. Then, we go to the Ashmore College campus to celebrate our new ink.

"You were right, Jeremy. I needed a tattoo. I will look at this tattoo for the rest of my life and think of my mom. It's like she is here with me always."

I lean over and kiss him in the car. Our relationship is stronger now that the trial is behind us, and we can just be ourselves everywhere we go.

Jeremy pulls the car onto the campus of Ashmore College. A big tree comes into view next to the student activity center. The tree has bigger branches and is a silver maple. The tree's center could fit five ambitious students who want to study together.

"Let's go check it out. It's called the study tree. Everyone studies there. I'm excited to come here with you next year. Are you excited about college?"

I nod. Jeremy was right. This is not the same tree my mother was murdered under. It's a different setting entirely. I climb the ladder and go into the tree. Jeremy follows behind me.

We both lean back and let the two-hundred-year-old tree hold us together in its safety. Jeremy fidgets in his pocket and pulls out a small box.

"Lily Green, I want to give you a promise ring. My parents dated throughout college. I know they aren't together anymore. But I think if we tried, maybe we could be. I want to give you this promise ring to let you know I will try my best to be here. I want to live and do my best to get better. I'm getting help, and it's because of you. You've done so much already for me. I wouldn't be who I am without you. I've decided to see my mom. I told her I wanted to talk about her boyfriends. I don't think she knows the truth of their abuse towards me, and she doesn't know how the divorce has made me angry. As we enter the last few weeks of school, I wanted to ask if you'd like to go to prom with me. I've already asked Mr.

Cronkwright, and he said we could go if you're comfortable. If that sounds lame, then I would like to take you on a date of your choosing. So, Lily Green, would you like to go to prom with me?"

I sit in the tree and look at Jeremy. Our relationship started in a tree. First, he was the dumb boy who tried to knock me out of the tree with his boots, and now, he wants me to go to prom. I never wanted to go to prom. It all sounded shallow and superficial to me. But for Jeremy, he is taking a huge step and is saying that he wants to live and experience prom with me. And for Jeremy, I can do anything.

"Yes, I would love to go to prom with you." Jeremy puts the promise ring on my finger. I don't honestly know what a promise ring means, but I know that I love Jeremy, and kissing him in a tree with a new tattoo on my arm is sexy. And being sexy as hell gives me all the feels inside.

The Funeral

It's time for the funeral. I've prepared a poem in memory of my mom. I'm nervous about sharing it and have asked Jeremy to read it if I start crying too much.

I'm glad Jeremy can attend the funeral like it's normal again. No police or criminal ankle bracelet. Mr. Davis will be attending the funeral as well. Amy and Tia had their own trials and are facing jail time like Kelly. Kelly got the longest sentence for life. Amy and Tia got twenty-five years if I heard the judge correctly. The KAT trio is all behind bars. This means there can be no disrespect at the funeral.

I put on the only black dress in the house. It's a black sundress. It's fitting that it belonged to mom. She was more into shopping, beauty, and vanity than I ever was.

I put my hair in a long French braid down my back. I haven't felt pretty in a long time—the sparrow pecks on the windowsill with its beak. I put birdseed out for it the night before. I'm glad to hear it and see if feeding today of all days. This sparrow is my mother's soul, and perhaps after today, she will never return to this window again. I like to think that this sparrow will fly into the clouds of heaven after today.

I wear black closed-toed shoes. No one but me will know the symbolism of close-toed shoes. It's me closing my grief off to the world. I know Jeremy will want to talk about how I am feeling. But I don't know how I am anymore. I have my mother's eyes and my father's heart. I carry her gaze in every mirror I see myself in.

I like what I see. Maybe this is how my mother saw me like I was prettier than I ever thought I was. The scrapbooks and photo albums she made will be displayed everywhere at her funeral. Even the scrapbook finished on her behalf will be there.

I'm nervous for everyone to see the display I've made on those pages. The truth is no one else, but I will know I ever finished it for her. Extensive collections of her photography days will be on display as well. She always enjoyed taking shots and photos of the sunset against lighthouses, the beach, and the mountains. Anywhere she would travel, a camera would always follow. The lens would zoom in and out on animals, plants, and the sky.

"Lily-kins, are you ready for today?" Dad asks. The only person to call me Lily-kins was mom. It was the nickname she blessed me with. Dad is using it now to see if I am ready to talk at her funeral. In many ways, sharing a poem at her funeral is more complicated than facing Kelly in a courtroom full of people.

No one is ready for a funeral. It's a party that comes with grief. It's when all the people who loved you in life gather and remember you. That's what will happen for mom. Her friends will come and remember her. And after today, that will be it. No more parties for her in her name. No more celebrating. I'm scared of the quiet that comes at the end of the funeral. The final silence means it really is the end of life.

The doorbell rings. It's Jeremy at the door. Seeing him without his anklet on is reassurance that some part of my life can become normal again. He's dressed up in a black suit. His dad is beside him, wearing a similar outfit.

I can't form words, and luckily for me, Jeremy picks up on this and hugs me.

"Lily, would you like me to read your poem for you today," Jeremy asks?

"Perhaps. I might. This is harder than a courtroom full of KAT trios."

I hand him the poem, and he scans the document. Then, he smiles and kisses my cheek. I guess he likes the simple message the poem states.

We all drive together to the funeral. Mom's photography classmates from years ago attend the funeral. The congregation of the Vineyard church is all there. Mr. Cronkwright and my former bus driver both attend as well.

Among the attendees is a face I was not expecting to see, a small woman who has the look of Kelly.

"Excuse me, ma'am, do I know you?" I ask.

"No. You don't. I'm Kelly's mom, Agatha Butterfield. I wanted to express my deepest sympathy from my family to yours. When I found out what...Kelly had done. What she was capable of. I was ashamed to call her my daughter. I am so sorry she ever did that to your family. I just wanted to let you know. I'm sorry."

It's startling to have Kelly's mom here. But I'm surprisedly not upset that she's here. The victim's family is never to blame for the bully's actions. And as for the bully, sometimes the parents of one have no idea. That's what I suspect to be accurate here. Kelly put a mask on for lots of people. It even worked in the same home she grew up in. So, I do the most unexpected thing. I hug her.

"Thanks for coming today."

Jeremy is shocked by my gesture. But what else was I supposed to do? Kicking out a funeral guest seems cruel. The mother of my mother's murderer is not the murderer herself. I remember seeing Agatha on the day of the trial. She was in tears, and her eyes never made eye contact with her daughter. She really was embarrassed to be her mother. In its cruel way, Kelly created an invisible bully that will follow her blood family wherever they go. They will be the family of the murderer of both Layla Green and Gerald McLaren. I almost feel sorry for Kelly's family. If I were them, I would turn my back on this town and start over somewhere else, under a brand-new alias provided by the police or government officials.

The grass is springy to jump on. It's been freshly watered. That's what I love about spring, the bouncy grass and flowers blooming everywhere. With graduation around the corner, I hardly have the strength to make another speech. I look at Jeremy and whisper that I need him to speak on my behalf.

Everyone sits down as the Pastor of the Vineyard church quotes the Bible. The sparrow from my windowsill sits in a nearby branch hovering over my mother's closed casket. It's my mother preparing to reach heaven with the angels.

Jeremy holds my hand as my father speaks. It's hard to concentrate on dad. He tells embarrassing stories of my childhood. How he met mom and how proud she'd be of me. Jeremy gets up on my behalf and walks over to the microphone next to the closed casket.

"Hello, everyone. I am Jeremy Davis, Lily's boyfriend. She asked me to read the following poem that she wrote on her behalf.

When the days are like morning and childhood sings,

I will remember how your cell phone rings,

When moments seem fleeting, and I still believe you'll always be there,

Who are you? You are my mom,
You won't get to see me preparing for prom,
But you will forever, always be mom,

When the skies become the night,
The morning sun will show its light,

I've found the wings of a sparrow that you will soon wear,
It's hard to see you when to me, your soul is everywhere,

When I miss your camera making a click,
The annoyance of saying 'cheese' made me tick,

I will miss our trips to the nearby pool,
We'd rather read books there and pretend to be cool,

I want to say goodbye one more time and cry with one more kiss,
Goodbye, my mother, it's you I will forever miss,

*When the storms fill my eyes, and all the feels make me cry,
I'll remember your sweet lullabies as I say, 'Goodbye.'"*

Jeremy leaves the microphone, and everyone next to me pats my back. I never knew what to say at funerals. Poems were the only words that made sense to me. Of course, they don't make sense to other people, but to me, that poem wasn't for them. The sparrow in the tree spreads its wings and flies out into the clouds. I know deep down that's the last time I will ever see that sparrow fly. But I enjoy its flight as I wave goodbye to my mother's soul one last time.

Dress Shopping

Prom has arrived. I don't have any girlfriends to go prom shopping with, and that's fine. Prom seems stupid to go to. It's not that I haven't thought about prom before. But I never imagined myself being pretty enough or worthy enough to go. Prom is for the lovely girls who get dolled up and look like models.

I'm the sexy librarian type. Sporting glasses and a romance novel while dancing is more my speed. I haven't told dad that I don't have a dress. I didn't want to give him one more thing to worry about. I've considered wearing one of mom's dresses and using her hair straightener. But, going into mom's closet will be hard because she is gone, and all the things a girl is supposed to do with their mom before prom is gone too.

The doorbell rings. It must be for dad since Jeremy is out with his mom today to have their *'come to Jesus-meeting'* about her abusive boyfriends.

"Hi, Lily." It's Mrs. Norris, my old bus driver. I saw her at the funeral but never did have a chance to say hello.

"Hi, Mrs. Norris. Thanks for stopping by. Thanks for coming to the funeral. Sorry I didn't say hello. I was overwhelmed with grief, as you know."

Mrs. Norris looks around the house and locks eyes with my father. He smiles at her, and she smiles back.

"Hello, Kathy. Thanks for coming," dad says as he opens the door wider for Mrs. Norris to enter.

"What is going on?" I ask because something is going on, and everyone but me seems to know what it is. I can't handle any more drama, bad news, or hospital visits.

"Well, Lily, I knew you wouldn't ask for a man's help with prom coming up. And with your sweet mother gone, I had to ask for another woman's help. So, when I saw Kathy at the funeral, it seemed like divine intervention."

I'm looking at both of them. My head goes back and forth between them. I shake my head in utter confusion. I still don't know what the hell he's trying to say.

"Can you speak English?" I ask.

"Yeah, sure. What I am trying to say, Lily is that I asked Kathy if she could take you prom dress shopping. And anything else you might need for prom tonight. I know it's tonight, and I haven't acknowledged it. Kathy has set up hair appointments for you and nails if that's what you want, sweetheart. I've decided to treat you like a princess before you go off to college. After all, you've been through with Jeremy, your mom, Kelly, school, and the courtroom. The least I can do is say *damn the price* so you and Jeremy can end your senior year the right way."

I'm stunned. I didn't expect dad to have time to think about me or silly prom. But, between Jeremy asking me to go and my dad going out of his financial means to pay for everything. I have to go and have a good time for both of them. So, I jump up and wrap my arms around my dad. I plant a large sloppy kiss on the top of his head.

"Are you ready to go then?" Mrs. Norris asks.

"Sure, Mrs. Norris. I'm as ready as I'll ever be."

"It's Kathy. You don't have to call me Mrs. Norris anymore. Especially since you'll be graduating soon."

"Okay, Miss Kathy, let's go get my hair done."

Miss Kathy rolls her eyes that I'm still uncomfortable not calling her by her first name. Just like Mr. Davis wants me to call him Benjamin. At what point in adulthood is one allowed to cross the line from calling someone

Mrs. This and Mr. That? After graduation, those titles might disappear unless you are a career person in a fancy company sitting behind a desk in a cubicle somewhere.

I've only had my hair done professionally once in my life. It was when I was nine years old. Mom and dad signed me up for the school talent show. They wanted me to recite my poems in front of an audience. Mom took me to *Roxanne's Salon* on 5th Avenue by the bypass a few hours before the talent show.

An old lady worked the cash register and gave large soda cans to the little kids. I had coke that day. I got my hair curled and waited impatiently for those hair torture devices to finish whatever voodoo they performed on my hair. I looked like a poodle and still managed to throw up in a nearby tuba. I never did recite my poems to the audience. I never liked audiences. Getting through the courtroom was a miracle. And thank God Jeremy read my poetry on my behalf at the funeral.

Today, Miss Kathy, or whatever her name is, is taking me back to *Roxanne's*. It's the most excellent hair salon for girls in town. I can't believe my dad is okay with spoiling me like this. When we enter the salon, I remember why I don't get my nails or hair done. The fumes of hell live in here. Every smell and every toxin I shouldn't breathe in exists in this room. It may look pleasant to the eyes, but the scent makes me want to run for the exit.

"Hello, you must be Lily." The old lady from my elementary years says. I can't believe she still works here.

I nod and follow the older woman to a salon chair. Kathy sits in the waiting room and rummages through old, damaged hair magazines. The ones with bad hairstyles go in all directions. Real people don't look like any of those pictures. All those models look eccentric and staged.

"Hello, Lily. I am Molly. What type of hair are you looking to get for prom today?"

I don't know much about hair. I hadn't even thought about styles.

"A braid crown," I say out loud. I remember reading about braid crowns in the history section of our Brit Lit textbook. They wore them a lot back then, or so they say.

"A braid crown," Molly repeats.

"Yeah, my boyfriend is really into them. He thinks he's Geoffrey Chaucer, the writer or something. He might be Shakespeare for all I know."

Molly smiles at my response. I might be getting girl-talk right because she is still laughing and smiling as she does origami to my hair. She tugs things, uses spray and bobby pins. After thirty minutes of tugging and small talk, my braid crown is done, and she has me look at myself in the mirror. For once, I like what I see. I don't look like my mom today. I usually see her face when I look in the mirror. Instead, I see a confident me. I am sure Jeremy will approve.

Kathy waltzes over and approves of my new look. I feel like Princess Mia from that old *Princess Diaries* movie. They transformed her look from poodle to queen during a three-minute song.

Kathy pays the old lady at the cash register and leaves Molly a tip. I find tipping and taxes to be confusing. When I was a kid and wanted a pair of shoes for $10, I didn't understand why they asked for more money. My parents always left cash for our waitresses as well at every restaurant. I'm still baffled by it as a senior in high school. Maybe it's only for the adultier-adults to understand.

Kathy and I get into the car, and she takes me to the mall. We go to a large dress shop inside. I find a nice long flowing purple halter top with glitter and lace on the bottom. It's the perfect dress to match my light-colored red hair. Kathy takes pictures as mom would have, and I can't help but cry a little.

"Can we take a selfie? I think mom would have wanted it." Kathy smiles. When my mom embarrassed me in front of all the Instagram kids and bus riding students, she was there. But despite that, I need to take a picture with my former bus driver now.

"Your mother would have wanted that picture. Let's take a few for a scrapbook and some for your social media."

I may not look like one of the cool kids hanging out with a bus driver. But it's so much more than that. It's me having a girls' outing with someone who has stood by me and has taken me to school year after year.

"Miss Kathy, can you come to my graduation?" I ask. She looks both flattered and surprised by my question.

"It would be my honor." I may not have a mother, but I have another role model in my life. Maybe, she can help encourage me as I head off to college in the fall. But, for now, I am happy to have a female role model in my life, and for once, taking pictures doesn't feel embarrassing. *Click!*

After Prom

My dad was right. I needed a girls' day after all the shit that has happened over this last year—especially these last few months. I'm not a good dancer. I can't be as bad as dad. It's rumored he fell during his wedding day dance. I'm not sure I believe him since there are no photos to back up the story.

Knowing mom, she would have insisted on photos being constantly clicked and taken. Every angle and every moment would have been captured. I've seen the wedding photos. There are no pictures of dad falling during his wedding dance.

I hate girl shoes. They go between your feet in unnatural ways, like flip flops, and make your heels ache. Beauty is painful. We have years of human history to back that up. My mom told me about the ancient Chinese performing a foot binding on their women's feet. I didn't understand what she meant until she showed a thirteen-year-old me the pictures of tiny shoes and broken feet. After she educated me, I was terrified of wearing lady's shoes. It is my prom day, and I am still fearful of wearing shoes that make my toes moan and ache.

Kathy takes me to a shoe department in a mall. Finally, I get a pair of worthy flats. There's no toe claustrophobia in their shoes. Kathy takes me home, and I thank her for all her help. It's nice to get a little pampered once in a while. I'm glad I let my dad talk me into this. He knew more than I did that I needed tending to.

Kathy takes me home. We don't spend long in the shoe department. I ring the doorbell, and dad smiles when he sees my fancy hair. I didn't get my nails done or make-up done. Instead, I decided to do my make-up. That I know how to do from my youthful years of being in theatre. I worked backstage a few times for the shows *Cats, Annie,* and *The Sound of Music.* I did make-up for all three. That was middle school and freshmen year. I haven't been in plays since. With college starting this fall, I hope my relationship with theatre will get rekindled with Jeremy.

I go to my room. I put on my prom attire and have several missed calls from Jeremy. So, I send him texts instead.

Me: Hey. Sorry, I am getting ready for prom.

Jeremy: Oh, fancy. Can I see?

Me: No, you can wait an hour. Where are we eating dinner?

Jeremy: Want to go to an Italian place?

Me: Sure. We can go to a drive-thru place for all I care.

Jeremy: I was thinking *Olive Garden*.

Me: Perfect. See you soon.

Jeremy. Bye. Love you.

Me: Love you too.

Our texts seem mature and cheesy at the same time. It's sometimes hard to believe that the boyfriend on the other side of those messages still struggles with suicidal thoughts. I know he is getting help and that he's come a long way. But sometimes, I am scared of all of his triggers. Jeremy doesn't know this, but I promised his dad I would keep an eye on him in college. I have a feeling he wants me to be his daughter-in-law someday. Who knows what direction we are heading in? I'm hopeful we'll be together a long time.

The next hour goes by slowly. I look through old scrapbooks of my mother the day she had her own prom. She looked as beautiful as ever. Dad takes a few pictures of me holding up mom's prom picture. It's almost like she is here with us, even though she isn't.

The doorbell rings. It's Jeremy wearing a tux. His black hair has gel in it. It's combed straight back. All of it is back except for a little piece that hangs at the side of his face. He's also shaved around the bottom edges of his head. I'm not used to Jeremy with a hot haircut and a tux. Although he takes one look at my glittery purple dress and hairstyle, he approves of me as well. My dad pulls out mom's camera and snaps all the pictures she would have taken. He takes some on his phone and sends them to Jeremy's dad.

"Have fun," dad says as he waves to us. I hug him. I don't want to seem like one of those insensitive teens who doesn't like their parents. Jeremy rented a fancy sports car from the car rental place to take me to prom. More like his dad rented it for Jeremy to use. It will be nice to go to prom in style.

"You look beautiful, Lily. Thanks for doing all of this for me."

"You're welcome. And Thanks. You look great too. Are you ready for dinner?" I ask.

"Yeah. I hope *Olive Garden's* okay. I ordered it ahead of time, actually. I want to pick it up. I want to take you somewhere before prom starts."

"Sure." I'm not going to argue with Jeremy, who needed me to come to prom. I'm going to hang on for the ride the entire evening and let him decide it all.

Jeremy opens the car door. He plays some version of 80s rock and roll. The windows roll down slightly, allowing the fresh spring air to leak into the car. Finally, we arrive at Ashmore College.

"Why are we at Ashmore College?" I ask.

"I told you we could do what we do best and hang out together in the big tree."

I'm not sure how to react. But I just go with it. Having a prom dinner in a tree sounds a bit random, but so like Jeremy. I take my lady shoes off and walk barefoot on the grass. I climb slowly into the big tree. Jeremy hands me the bag of food. I stick my phone in my bra. Dresses need pockets. Mom and I used to argue over that. Jeremy watches me stick my phone down my bra and blushes slightly. He climbs up slowly, trying not to rip the tux.

"Did you rent the tux?" I ask.

"No, it's my cousin Lance's. He gave it to me to keep the other day. Thanks for coming here with me. I wanted to get fresh air before prom. A stuffy restaurant with people staring at us made me nervous. That's why I started sitting in trees in the first place. I didn't like people looking at me, and then I noticed all of them looking down at their phones. The world above them all is free of their gazing eyes."

That's why he was like Mr. Chaucer, people-watching. He really did see people more than they saw themselves, especially me.

"We can hang in this tree as long as you'd like next school year."

"That will be nice. Also, I got a job at the zoo. They liked the community service I did. So, they offered me a summer job helping their staff tend to the animals."

"That's great news, Jeremy. You'll love that. How did it go talking with your mother the other night?"

The joy on his face about the zoo job leaves.

"We did talk. She's glad I am in counseling, but she still fails to see why I don't feel safe with her dumb boyfriend. I told her I was staying with dad the rest of the year. She understands. It's not perfect, but we both came to an understanding. That's good enough for me."

He grabs my hand as a breeze dances in the tree. I take a few selfies of us eating spaghetti in our prom attire with tree branches protecting us. We finish our spaghetti and wipe our faces clean. A nearby runner offers to take our picture beneath the tree. I hand my phone over, and we smile at several funny pictures. The spirit of mom comes to me with that runner.

Then an idea hits me. I see the small campus lake away from the big tree. A small dock clings to the edges of a small lake. I take Jeremy's hand and lead us to the side of the pier.

"What are you doing? The prom is going to start soon. So, we'll be late."

"No, we won't. I have an idea." I pull out my cell phone and play a slow dance playlist. I turn the volume up and walk us onto the dock. Jeremy smiles and follows me. I know I wanted to follow Jeremy's lead tonight, but he doesn't like people staring at him. He said so himself. Here on a dock away from people is where we can dance and be away from everyone.

Jeremy puts his cheek on mine as we start to slow dance to the music on my phone.

"You're right. I like this better. Let's just stay here tonight and dance."

I smile in agreement. Jeremy dances with me for a long time on the docks of Ashmore College. The sunsets and he kisses me. Finally, the stars come out, and we are still dancing. Perhaps I can like prom night after all. Jeremy smells my hair. The evening is getting later, and Jeremy is sick of dancing.

He goes into the *Olive Garden* bag and pulls out a chocolate cake for dessert. We eat it on the dock. The chocolate slides down my throat.

"Oh, now that's some good cake."

"I know, right?" Jeremy agrees.

We finish the cake. Jeremy kisses me, takes the trash out of my hands, and sets it in the bag. Jeremy and I never discussed what we would do after prom. Everyone always talks about it in secret, but never do they plan it. I decide to let him take me wherever he wants.

"Want to go watch a movie at my house?" He asks.

"Sure," I reply as I take his hand. Our fingers interlock. He pulls me into his arms, and his lips touch the tips of my ears.

"I have a present for you at the house." His whisper touches my hair like a passing wind.

We walk to his car and get to his house in fifteen minutes. My heart rate picked up immensely during that car ride.

I follow Jeremy up the steps of his front porch. The door squeaks behind me, and Mr. Davis waves at us.

"Well, don't you all look nice. Help yourself to the brownies I've just made." The thought of eating more chocolate sounds excellent. So, I help myself to a small slice.

"Dad, I wanted to show Lily the movie." His eyes get big as they have a conversation with their eyes. Jeremy's dad puts a DVD in, and on the screen pops up pictures of us and all the things we've done together as a couple. A little song plays in the background as the slides continue.

"This is so thoughtful, Jeremy. Thank you, I love it." I jump into Jeremy's arms and kiss him some more. Mr. Davis uses that as his cue to leave the room.

"Stay as long as you'd like, Lily," Mr. Davis says as I give him the thumbs up. Then, he goes to his room and shuts the door.

Jeremy and I sit and watch *Ironman 2*. I never saw the first one, but I read the comics occasionally with dad. So, I'm sure I can figure the plot out. Finally, the credits roll on the screen, and Jeremy leads me to his room, where the after-prom will begin.

Jeremy closes his door behind him and starts taking his shirt off in front of me. We've had sex before, but it's different now. Time has passed between us, and I just sit on the bed. Since our last encounter, mom has died, Jeremy almost committed suicide, and he's been to jail.

"What's wrong, Lily?" Jeremy says as he sits next to me.

"The last time we had sex, cops came over and took you away from me," I say. So I think, in some ways, I have a slight panic attack.

"It will be fine. Kelly's in prison, not me. Remember how hard Officer Reynolds worked to help prove my innocence?"

'You're right. I was just a little shaken thinking about it."

"I love you, Lily. I hope you know that."

"I love you too, Jeremy. And yes, I do know that." His lips touch mine and the world spins. The troubles of the world fade away as my dress slips off. We slip into the world of the after-prom and make love on his bed. Only this time, I know that Jeremy and I will wake up with no regrets and no cops to greet us. Instead, we will wake up in a place where we can love with all the feels, and that's when I know being in love really can last forever.

Graduation Day

The following week flies by. And despite taking classes online to wrap up my senior year, I will miss Mr. Cronkwright. He will be the speaker for our high school graduation. In addition, he's been nominated to win the teacher of the year award. I am sure he will win.

Our graduation gowns are black with a maroon-colored tassel. My dad has been acting emotional around me since prom ended. With one week between prom and graduation day, I can't say I blame him. This has been hard without my mom to help. It's been an adjustment for him. Her absence won't disappear overnight.

I put my graduation gown on. It's a long sweaty thing. I look like a Hogwarts student. If you gave me a wand, I could teach magic in the fall. Dad has this habit of taking photos on my mother's behalf. So I promised him I would finish my high school scrapbooks in mom's place.

The doorbell rings. It's Jeremy in his matching outfit. Both of his parents are with him. They've managed to set aside their differences for his graduation day. It's the first time I've seen Jeremy's mom. I've heard enough about her. I feel like I have a sense of who she is as a person. Her long curly brown hair has grey strands poking out in all directions. At least his mom is alive.

"Hello, Jeremy's mom. I am Lily." She shakes my hand and pulls me in for a hug.

"Hi, I am Kayla. Thanks for helping Jeremy with everything. He told me all about you a few weeks ago. Our family can't thank you enough for...well, you know what you did. And congrats to both of you."

Jeremy smiles, and our silly-looking graduation hats cover up his new haircut. I'm excited to see him with it off later. When it's off, we will get to toss them into the air. I get to sit two seats down from Jeremy during the ceremony. Only Elizabeth Chesterton and Fred Douglass will be between us as they call our names during the ceremony.

Time flies, and I find myself in my graduation chair. Our small class of 100 students all match and look like a sea of black costumes in chairs. Mr. Cronkwright takes the microphone as the principal awards him with the teacher of the year award. He takes the awards and accepts them graciously.

Mr. Cronkwright gives an important speech. It's hard to pay attention when I am so nervous to walk onto the stage and be cheered for. His speech has something mentioning the famous book, *Oh the Places You'll Go* in it. It's the book everyone who graduates gets as a present. Dr. Seuss probably never intended this book to be for graduation. It just happened that way.

Jeremy's name is called. He stands up and walks across the stage. I jump and clap and watch him receive his diploma. His parents blow horns in all directions. His mom wears a foam finger. I turn back, and his mother is hugging his dad. Jeremy gets off the stage and waits to the side as Elizabeth Chesterton and Fred Douglass graduate.

My name is called, and my heart pounds. Mr. Cronkwright smiles and hands me my diploma. I get a pat on the back. Dad takes a million pictures as I turn to see him. I hold my diploma high in the air for mom to see. I take the steps down the stairs and am greeted by a happy Jeremy.

The happiness on his face tells me all I need to know about the future. Our emotions will carry us into a better tomorrow. We have cried together, been enemies, and have become best friends. No matter how I feel about Jeremy later, I love him more than I ever have. And loving someone like Jeremy is an honor that has all the feels to go with it.

About the Author

Holly Hamilton

Holly Hamilton loves writing novels in the Young Adult, Romance, and New Adult genres. She currently lives in Michigan with her husband, Matt, and two young children. She enjoys going on hikes, drinking hot chocolate, and going camping in her free time. While growing up, Holly discovered her love of writing at a fine arts camp she attended in Indiana. Holly is also a stay-at-home-mother, former teacher, and current homeschool teacher.

www.ingramcontent.com/pod-product-compliance
Lightning Source LLC
LaVergne TN
LVHW041712070526
838199LV00045B/1310